THE DARK TOWER
AND OTHER STORIES

BY C. S. LEWIS

THE PILGRIM'S REGRESS
THE PROBLEM OF PAIN
THE SCREWTAPE LETTERS
AND SCREWTAPE PROPOSES A TOAST
BROADCAST TALKS
THE ABOLITION OF MAN
CHRISTIAN BEHAVIOUR
BEYOND PERSONALITY
THE GREAT DIVORCE
GEORGE MACDONALD: AN ANTHOLOGY
MIRACLES
TRANSPOSITION AND OTHER ADDRESSES
MERE CHRISTIANITY
SURPRISED BY JOY
REFLECTIONS ON THE PSALMS
THE WORLD'S LAST NIGHT AND OTHER ESSAYS
THE FOUR LOVES
LETTERS TO MALCOLM: CHIEFLY ON PRAYER
POEMS
OF OTHER WORLDS
LETTERS OF C. S. LEWIS
NARRATIVE POEMS

For Children
THE LION, THE WITCH AND THE WARDROBE
PRINCE CASPIAN
THE VOYAGE OF THE DAWN TREADER
THE SILVER CHAIR
THE HORSE AND HIS BOY
THE MAGICIAN'S NEPHEW
THE LAST BATTLE

Fiction
OUT OF THE SILENT PLANET
PERELANDRA
THAT HIDEOUS STRENGTH
TILL WE HAVE FACES
THE DARK TOWER AND OTHER STORIES

C. S. Lewis

THE DARK TOWER

AND OTHER STORIES

EDITED BY
WALTER HOOPER

A Harvest/HBJ Book
Harcourt Brace Jovanovich, Publishers
San Diego   New York   London

Requests for permission to make copies of any part of the work
should be mailed to: Permissions, Harcourt Brace Jovanovich,
Publishers, Orlando, FL 32887.

Printed in the United States of America

"The Shoddy Lands" was first published in *The Magazine of Fan-
tasy and Science Fiction*, X (February 1956). "Ministering Angels"
was first published in *The Magazine of Fantasy and Science Fiction*,
XIII (January 1958). "Forms of Things Unknown" and "After
Ten Years" were first published in *Of Other Worlds*: *Essays and
Stories*, by C. S. Lewis, copyright © 1966 by the Trustees of the
Estate of C. S. Lewis.

Library of Congress Cataloging in Publication Data

Lewis, Clive Staples, 1898-1963.
The dark tower, and other stories.

CONTENTS: Hooper, W. Preface.—The dark tower,
with a note by W. Hooper.—The man born blind. [etc.]
I. Title.
PZ3.L58534Dar8   [PR6023.E926]   823'.9'12   76-52387
ISBN 0-15-123902-9
ISBN 0-15-623930-2 pbk.

G H I J

Contents

Preface

C. S. Lewis died on 22 November 1963. In January 1964
I went to stay with Dr and Mrs Austin Farrer at Keble
College while Lewis's brother, Major W. H. Lewis, began
clearing out the Kilns (the family home) preparatory to
moving into a smaller house, where I was later to join
him. The Lewis brothers felt little of that veneration for
manuscripts so typical of many of us, and Major Lewis,
after setting aside those papers which had a special
significance for him, began disposing of the others. Thus
it was that a great many things which I was never able
to identify found their way on to a bonfire which burned
steadily for three days. Happily, however, the Lewis's
gardener, Fred Paxford, knew that I had the highest
regard for anything in the master's hand, and when he
was given a great quantity of C. S. Lewis's notebooks
and papers to lay on the flames, he urged the Major to
delay till I should have a chance to see them. By what
seems more than coincidence, I appeared at the Kilns
that very day and learned that unless I carried the papers
away with me that afternoon they would indeed be
destroyed. There were so many that it took all my
strength and energy to carry them back to Keble College.

That evening, while glancing through them, I came
across a manuscript which excited me very much. Yellow
with age but still perfectly legible, it opened with the
words: ' "Of course," said Orfieu, "the sort of time-
travelling you read about in books – time-travelling in the
body – is absolutely impossible." ' A few lines down the page
I came across the name of 'Ransom', whom it said 'had
been the hero, or victim, of one of the strangest adventures
that had ever befallen a mortal man'. I knew I was reading
part of another of Lewis's interplanetary novels – *The*

7

Dark Tower as I have called it – which is published here for the first time.

Those already familiar with Lewis's interplanetary trilogy, *Out of the Silent Planet* (1938), *Perelandra* (1943) and *That Hideous Strength* (1945), will recall that the first of these novels ends with a letter from the fictional Dr Elwin Ransom of Cambridge to his friend C. S. Lewis (himself a minor character in the stories). After remarking that his enemy, Weston, had 'shut the door' to space-travel through the heavens, he ends his letter (and the book) with the statement that 'the way to the planets lies through the past' and that 'if there is to be any more space-travelling, it will have to be time-travelling as well . . . !'

During the brief period that I was his secretary, Lewis told me that he never at any time had any intention of writing three connecting novels or creating what some see as a single coherent 'myth'. I believe, however, that though he thought he was completely rid of his antagonists, Weston and Devine, he had in mind the possibility of a sequel to *Out of the Silent Planet* in which Ransom would play some part and in which time-travel would figure pretty largely – as is evidenced by the obvious tie-up between the last sentence of *Out of the Silent Planet* and the opening sentence of *The Dark Tower*. Indeed, this is borne out by a letter to Sister Penelope CSMV dated 9 August 1939 in which he says that the 'letter' at the end of *Out of the Silent Planet* and ' "the circumstances which put the book out of date" are merely a way of preparing a sequel'. My guess is that Lewis began writing the story almost immediately after completing *Out of the Silent Planet* in 1938, and this would appear to be supported by the passage on page 19 where MacPhee, growing impatient with the talk about time-travel, chaffs Orfieu about the 'remarkable discovery' that 'a man in 1938 can't get to 1939 in less than a year'.

The manuscript of *The Dark Tower* consists of 62 sheets of ruled paper measuring $8\frac{1}{2}'' \times 13''$ and numbered

8

from 1 to 64. Pages 11 and 49 are missing, and – sadly – the story is incomplete. It breaks off in mid-sentence on page 64, and as I have never discovered any more pages I cannot be certain whether or not Lewis ever finished it. As it is best saved till later, I have included all that I have been able to learn about the story in a note, appended to the end of the fragment.

There are those who feel there is something cruel in publishing fragments because in many cases we cannot even guess how the author would have ended his story. That is one reason why I advised Lewis's trustees to hold on to *The Dark Tower* for the time being. Another is that I anticipate unfavourable comparisons .with the trilogy. Notwithstanding the high expectations established by Lewis's pen, I nevertheless do not believe that an artifact such as *The Dark Tower* should be expected to approach the invention and completed perfection of his superb interplanetary trilogy. We must suppose even Lewis to have believed this: he had never attempted to publish it, and, considering his great fecundity, I dare say he had long forgotten having written it. But one thing he would not have forgotten, and that is the unwisdom of mistaking the publication of what was intended as little more than a literary diversion for the advancement of an ethical theorem. The world is not sinking under the weight of good holiday fiction, and what it would be madness to treat with that unfortunate seriousness which puts literature on a level with Scripture, it is a pleasure to offer as entertainment.

The next piece in this book, 'The Man Born Blind', was found in one of the notebooks given me by Lewis's brother. It has never been published before and, as far as I know, was not seen by anyone during the author's lifetime with the exception of Owen Barfield and possibly J. R. R. Tolkien. Though I regret never having asked Tolkien about the story, I was interested to learn that he mentioned it to Professor Clyde S. Kilby who says in *Tolkien and the Silmarillion* (1976): 'Tolkien told me of C. S. Lewis's story about the man born with a cataract

9

on each eye. He kept hearing people talk of light but could not understand what they meant. After an operation he had some sight but had not yet come to understand *light*. Then one day he saw a haze rising from a pond (actually, said Tolkien, the pond at the front of Lewis's home) and thought that at last he was seeing light. In his eagerness to experience real light, he rushed joyfully into it and was drowned' (pp. 27-8). As there is no mention in the story as to what caused the man's blindness (some children are indeed born with cataracts) and the man is not drowned, it seems likely that Tolkien heard Lewis tell a version of the story rather than that he read the one published here. Owen Barfield tells me that 'The Man Born Blind' was written during the late 1920s when he and Lewis were deep in that 'Great War' debate over Appearance and Reality which Lewis refers to in his autobiography, *Surprised by Joy*. Though the story is perfectly clear, the 'idea' behind it was later taken a bit further in Lewis's essay 'Meditation in a Toolshed' in which he discusses the fatal modern habit of always looking *at* things, such as a beam of light, rather than not only *at* them but *along* them to the objects which they illumine. Another possible motivation for the story may have been Lewis's fascination with the account of the man born blind in St Mark (8:23-5), where it is recorded that Jesus 'took the blind man by the hand and led him out of the town; and when he had spit on his eyes, and put his hands upon him, he asked him if he saw aught. And he looked up, and said, I see men as trees, walking. After that he put his hands again upon his eyes, and made him look up: and he was restored, and saw every man clearly.'

Mr Barfield has said in his introduction to *Light on C. S. Lewis* (1965) that Lewis, some time after showing the story to him, 'told me . . . he had been informed by an expert that the acquisition of sight by a blind adult was not in fact the shattering experience he had imagined for the purposes of his story. Years later I found in one of Sir Julian Huxley's books an allusion to the initial results of such an operation, which suggested that Lewis had in fact imagined them pretty accurately' (p. xviii). Certainly Lewis kept *trying* to imagine the results more accurately. The story was written on the right-hand pages of one of his notebooks. On the left-hand pages, in a script penned some years later, are revisions of those portions which describe what the protagonist expected Light to look like. Unluckily, these revised portions cannot be linked together with the rest of the original version and I have had to content myself with publishing the original, and only complete version of the story there is.

Lewis was not fond of that chaotic genre of stories which go under the name of 'stream of consciousness' literature – or *'steam* of consciousness' as I have heard him call it – because he believed it impossible for the human mind to observe its thoughts and be the object of its thoughts at the same time. This would be like looking in a mirror to see what you look like when you are not looking at yourself. Still, he thought it would be fun to pretend he was doing something like this, and the result is 'The Shoddy Lands', which appeared first in the *Magazine of Fantasy and Science Fiction*, X (February 1956), and afterwards in his *Of Other Worlds: Essays and Stories* (1966).

'Ministering Angels' was written in answer to Dr Robert S. Richardson's article 'The Day after We Land on Mars', which was published in the *Saturday Review* (28 May 1955). Dr Richardson put forward the serious suggestion that 'if space travel and colonization of the planets eventually become possible on a fairly large scale, it seems probable that we may be forced into first tolerating and finally openly accepting an attitude toward sex that is taboo in our present social framework . . . To put it bluntly, may it not be necessary for the success of the project to send some nice girls to Mars at regular intervals to relieve tensions and promote morale?' Just what those 'nice girls' are apt to be like, and the kind of 'morale' they will promote is the subject of Lewis's delightful 'Ministering Angels', which was published in the *Magazine of Fantasy and Science Fiction*, XIII (January 1958), and afterwards in *Of Other Worlds*.

Long before anyone set foot on the Moon, Lewis had predicted that 'the real Moon, if you could reach it and survive, would in a deep and deadly sense be just like anywhere else . . . No man would find an abiding strangeness on the Moon unless he were the sort of man who could find it in his own back garden.' Besides the so to speak indigenous strangeness Lewis imagined for Mars in *Out of the Silent Planet* and Venus in *Perelandra*, he has Ransom ask, 'Were all the things which appeared as mythology on earth scattered through other worlds as realities?'

It was partly an answer to this question which furnished Lewis with a subject for his story 'Forms of Things Unknown', the manuscript of which I discovered among the papers given me by Major Lewis. Lewis may have decided against publishing it because he supposed that many of his readers would not be familiar enough with classical mythology to take his point. However, rather than give the 'point' away, and possibly spoil the surprise ending, I have decided to reprint the story just as it originally appeared in *Of Other Worlds*.

After Ten Years is, like *The Dark Tower*, a fragment of what was intended to be a full-length novel, and is reprinted from *Of Other Worlds*. Lewis mentioned the idea of the book to Roger Lancelyn Green in 1959, and the first four chapters were completed soon after this. The story began, as Lewis said of his science-fiction trilogy and the seven *Chronicles of Narnia*, with 'seeing pictures' in his head. His time and sympathy were almost completely absorbed at this period in nursing his ill and much-loved wife. By the time she died, shortly after their trip to Greece in 1960, Lewis's health was broken, and the well-spring of his inspiration – 'seeing pictures' – nearly dried up. He persevered, nevertheless, and was able to write one more chapter. Roger Lancelyn Green, Alastair Fowler and I, with whom Lewis discussed the story, believed that it could be one of his finest and we urged him to go on with it. No more 'pictures' were forthcoming, but the itch to write was still there and he paid me the highest compliment ever to come my way in asking what I should like him to write. I begged for 'a romance – something on the order of his science-fiction novels', to which he replied that there was no market for this kind of thing those days. England, and a great many other countries, were in the grip of 'slice of life realism' during the early 1960s and even Lewis could not foresee what an enormous, almost cataclysmic, effect his friend Tolkien's fantasies were soon to have upon literature and our very understanding of reality itself, or the steadily increasing hold which his own would take. In any event, Lewis could get no further with his story before he died.

As far as I know, Lewis wrote only one draft of *After Ten Years*, the manuscript of which was, again, one of those saved from the fire. Lewis did not divide the fragments into parts (or give it a title), but as each 'chapter' appears to have been written at a different time, I have decided to retain these rather natural divisions. I must warn the reader, however, that what I have called Chapter 5 does not really follow Chapter 4. The author was anticipating the end of the story. Had he completed it, there would have been many chapters between 4 and 5.

Lewis discussed this work in some detail with Roger Lancelyn Green and Alastair Fowler, and I have asked them to write about the conversation they had with him. The nature of the story – especially the brilliant 'twist' which comes at the end of the first chapter – makes it imperative that the reader save their notes until last.

It has long been the dream of many people to see C. S. Lewis's unpublished and uncollected fiction in a single volume, which could be placed alongside all his other romances. Those other works (excepting, of course, Lewis's unpublished juvenilia) are readily available in English and a good many foreign translations as well, and consist of *Out of the Silent Planet, Perelandra, That*

Hideous Strength, the seven *Chronicles of Narnia*, and *Till We Have Faces*. Those who have these books on their shelves will, by the addition of *The Dark Tower and Other Stories*, own the complete fiction of C. S. Lewis.

A book, once I have read and handled it, has always seemed to me an inevitable part of life – an open-and-shut case of fact, the origins of which grow dimmer as time passes. Before this book hardens into a seeming inevitability, I want to record my indebtedness to my fellow trustees of the Lewis Estate, Owen Barfield and the late A. C. Harwood, and my other good friends, Gervase Matthew (who also died while this book was in preparation), R. E. Havard, Colin and Christian Hardie, Roger Lancelyn Green and Alastair Fowler, all of whom knew Lewis longer than I. In this free-wheeling age it is not always easy to get people to believe that one is not diminished by seeking advice from one's natural superiors, but I have a distinct sense of having grown as a result of the help and kindness Owen Barfield and others have given me in editing these stories.

Oxford   WALTER HOOPER

THE DARK TOWER

'Of course,' said Orfieu, 'the sort of time-travelling you read about in books – time-travelling in the body – is absolutely impossible.'

There were four of us in Orfieu's study. Scudamour, the youngest of the party, was there because he was Orfieu's assistant. MacPhee had been asked down from Manchester because he was known to us all as an inveterate sceptic, and Orfieu thought that if once he were convinced, the learned world in general would have no excuse for incredulity. Ransom, the pale man with the green shade over his grey, distressed-looking eyes, was there for the opposite reason – because he had been the hero, or victim, of one of the strangest adventures that had ever befallen a mortal man. I had been mixed up with that affair – the story is told in another book – and it was to Ransom I owed my presence in Orfieu's party. With the exception of MacPhee, we might be described as a secret society : that sort of society whose secrets need no passwords, oaths, or concealment because they automatically keep themselves. Unconquerable misunderstanding and unbelief defends them from the public, or, if you will, shelters the public from them. Much more work of this kind goes on than is commonly supposed, and the most important events in every age never reach the history books. All three of us knew, and Ransom had actually experienced, how thin is the crust which protects 'real life' from the fantastic.

'Absolutely impossible?' said Ransom. 'Why?'

'I bet *you* see,' said Orfieu, glancing towards MacPhee.

'Go on, go on,' said the Scot with the air of one refusing to interrupt children at their play. We all echoed him.

'Well,' said Orfieu, 'time-travelling clearly means going into the future or the past. Now where will the particles that compose your body be five hundred years hence? They'll be all over the place – some in the earth, some in plants and animals, and some in the bodies of your descendants, if you have any. Thus, to go to the year 3000 AD means going to a time at which your body doesn't exist; and that means, according to one hypothesis, becoming nothing, and, according to the other, 'becoming a disembodied spirit.'

'But half a moment,' said I, rather foolishly, 'you don't need to find a body waiting for you in the year 3000. You would take your present body with you.'

'But don't you see that's just what you can't do?' said Orfieu. 'All the matter which makes up your body now will be being used for different purposes in 3000.'

I still gaped.

'Look here,' he said. 'You will grant me that the same piece of matter can't be in two different places at the same time. Very well. Now, suppose that the particles which at present make up the tip of your nose by the year 3000 form part of a chair. If you could travel to the year 3000 and, as you suggest, take your present body with you, that would mean that at some moment in 3000 the very same particles would have to be both in your nose and in the chair – which is absurd.'

'But aren't the particles in my nose changing all the time anyway?' said I.

'Quite, quite,' said Orfieu. 'But that doesn't help. You'll have to have *some* particles to make a nose in 3000 if you're going to have a body then. And all the particles in the universe by 3000 will already be employed in other ways – doing their own jobs.'

'In other words, sir,' said Scudamour to me, 'there are no spare particles to be had in the universe at any given moment. It's like trying to get back into college after you've gone down : all the rooms are occupied as they were in your time, but by different people.'

'Always assuming,' said MacPhee, 'that there is no real addition to the total matter of the universe going on.'

'No,' said Orfieu, 'only assuming that no appreciable addition of new matter to this planet goes on in the very complicated way, and at the great pace, which would be required by Lewis's hypothesis. You agree with what I've been saying, I suppose?'

'Oh certainly, certainly,' said MacPhee slowly, and rolling his r's. 'I never thought there was any kind of travelling in time except the sort we're all doing already – I mean, travelling into the future at the rate of sixty minutes an hour whether you like it or not. It would interest me more if you could find a way of *stopping* it.'

'Or going back,' said Ransom with a sigh.

'Going back comes up against the same difficulty as going forward, sir,' said Scudamour. 'You couldn't have a body in 1500 any more than in 3000.'

There was a moment's pause. Then MacPhee spoke with a slow smile.

'Well, Dr Orfieu,' he said, 'I'll away back to Manchester tomorrow and tell them that the University of Cambridge has made a remarkable discovery; namely, that a man in 1938 can't get to 1939 in less than a year, and that dead bodies lose their noses. And I'll add that their arguments completely satisfied me.'

The jibe recalled Orfieu to the real purpose of our meeting, and after a few moments of keen but not unkindly chaff between the two philosophers we settled ourselves to listen again.

'Well,' said Orfieu, 'the argument that we have just gone through convinced me that any kind of "time machine", anything that would take your body to another time, was intrinsically impossible. If we are to have experience of times before our birth and after our death it must be done in some quite different way. If the thing is possible it must consist in looking at another time while we ourselves remain here – as we look at the stars through telescopes while we remain on the earth. What one wants, in fact, is not a sort of time flying-machine but something which does to time what the telescope does to space.'

'A *chronoscope* in fact,' suggested Ransom.

'Exactly – thanks for the word; a chronoscope. But that wasn't my first idea. The first thing I thought of, when I had abandoned the false trail of a time machine, was the possibility of mystical experience. You needn't grin, Mac-Phee; you ought to cultivate an open mind. At any rate I had an open mind. I saw that in the writings of the mystics we had an enormous body of evidence, coming from all sorts of different times and places – and often quite independently – to show that the human mind has a power, under certain conditions, of rising to experience outside the normal time-sequence. But this, too, proved to be a false trail. I don't mean merely that the preliminary exercises seemed extraordinarily difficult and, indeed, involved a complete abandonment of one's normal life. I mean that the further I looked into it the more clearly I saw that the mystical experience took you out of time altogether – into the timeless, not into other times, which was what I wanted; now – and what's amusing *you*, Ransom?'

'Excuse me,' said Ransom. 'But it is funny, you know. The idea of a man thinking he could become a saint as a minor detail in his scientific training. You might as well imagine you could use the stairs of heaven as a short cut to the nearest tobacconist's. Don't you see that long before you had reached the level of timeless experience you would have had to become so interested in something else – or, frankly, Someone Else – that you wouldn't be bothering about time-travel?'

'Um – well, perhaps,' said Orfieu. 'I hadn't thought of it in that light. Well, anyway, for the reasons I've just mentioned, I decided that mysticism was useless for my purpose. It was only then it occurred to me that the real secret was much nearer home. You know the enormous difficulties in any physiological explanation of memory? And you may have heard that on metaphysical grounds there is a good deal to be said for the theory that memory is direct perception of the past. I came to the conclusion that this theory was right – that when we remember, we are not simply getting the result of something that goes on inside our heads. We are directly experiencing the past.'

'In that case,' said MacPhee, 'it is very remarkable that

we remember only those bits of it which fall within our own lives and have affected our own physical organisms.' (He pronounced it 'arganism'.)

'It would be very remarkable,' replied Orfieu, 'if it were true. But it isn't. If you'd read the story of the two English ladies at Trianon with an open mind, MacPhee, you would know that there is on record at least one indisputable instance in which the subjects saw a whole scene from a part of the past long before their birth. And if you had followed up that hint, you would have found the real explanation of all the so-called ghost-stories which people like you have to explain away. And by that time it might have dawned on you that there is a great deal in your mental picture of, say, Napoleon or Pericles, which you can't remember reading in any book but which agrees in the oddest way with the things that other people imagine about them. But I won't go on. You can look at my notes for yourself after dinner. I, at any rate, am perfectly satisfied that our experience of the past – what you call "memory" – is not limited to our own lives.'

'At least you'll admit,' said I, 'that we remember our own lives much more often than anything else.'

'No, I don't admit even that. It seems that we do, and I can explain why it must seem so.'

'Why?' said Ransom.

'Because the fragments of our own lives are the only fragments of the past which we recognize. When you get a mental picture of a little boy called Ransom in an English public school you at once label it "memory" because you know you *are* Ransom and were at an English public school. When you get a picture of something that happened ages before your birth, you call it imagination; and in fact most of us at present have no test by which to distinguish real fragments of the past from mental fictions. It was by a bit of amazing luck that the ladies at Trianon were able to find objective checks which proved that what they had seen was part of the real past. A hundred cases of the same kind might occur without such checks (in fact, they do) and the subjects merely conclude that they have been dreaming or had an hallucination. And then, naturally, they keep quiet about it.'

'And the future?' said MacPhee. 'You're not going to say that we "remember" it too?'

'We wouldn't call it remembering,' said Orfieu, 'for memory means perception of the past. But that we see the future is perfectly certain. Dunne's book proved that –'

MacPhee gave a roar like a man in pain.

'It's all very well, MacPhee,' Orfieu continued, 'but the only thing that enables you to jeer at Dunne is the fact that you have refused to carry out the experiments he suggests. If you had carried them out you would have got the same results that he got, and I got, and everyone got who took the trouble. Say what you like, but the thing is proved. It's as certain as any scientific truth whatever.'

'But look here, Orfieu,' said I, 'there must be some sense in which we *don't* see the future. I mean – well, hang it all, who's going to win the boatrace this year?'

'Cambridge,' said Orfieu. (I was the only Oxford man present.) 'But, to be serious, I'm not saying that you can see all the future, nor that you can pick out those bits of the future you happen to choose. You can't do that with the present – you don't know what money I have in my pocket at this moment, or what your own face looks like, or even, apparently, where your matches are.' (He handed me his own box.) 'All I mean is that of the innumerable things going through your mind at any moment, while some are mere imagination, some are real perceptions of the past and others real perceptions of the future. You don't recognize most of the past ones and, of course, you recognize *none* of the future.'

'But we ought to recognize them when they arrive; that is, when they become the present,' said MacPhee.

'How do you mean?' asked Ransom.

'Well,' said MacPhee, 'if I'd had a mental picture last week of this room and all you fellows sitting there, I grant you I should not have recognized it *then* as a picture of the future. But now that I'm really here, I ought to remember that I had a prevision of it last week. And that never happens.'

'It does happen,' said Orfieu. 'And that explains the feeling we often have that something which we are now experiencing has all happened before. In fact this occurs so often that it has become the basis for the religion of half the world – I mean, the belief in reincarnation – and of all theories of the Eternal Recurrence, like Nietzsche's.'

'It never happens to me,' said MacPhee stoutly.

'Perhaps not,' said Orfieu, 'but it does to thousands of people. And there is a reason why we notice it so little. If there is one thing that Dunne has proved up to the hilt it is that there is some law in the mind which actually forbids us to notice it. In his book he gives you a series of examples of an event in real life resembling an event in a dream. And the funny thing is that if the real event comes first, you see the resemblance at once; but if the dream comes first, you just ignore it until it is pointed out to you.'

'That,' said MacPhee drily, 'is a very remarkable law.'

'Try his examples,' said Orfieu. 'They're irresistible.'

'Obviously,' said Ransom, 'there must be such a law if we are going to have the experience of living in time at all. Or, rather, it's the other way round. The fact of having minds that work like that is what puts us into time.'

'Exactly,' said Orfieu. 'Well, if we once agree that the mind is intrinsically capable of perceiving the past and the future directly – however much it suppresses and limits the power in order to be a human mind and to live in time – what is the next step? We know that all the mind's perceptions are exercised by means of the body. And we have discovered how to extend them by means of instruments, as we extend our sight by the telescope or, in another sense, by the camera. Such instruments are really artificial *organs*, copied from the natural organs: the lens is a copy of the eye. To make a similar instrument for our time-perceptions we must find the time-organ and then copy it. Now I claim to have isolated what I call the Z substance in the human brain. On the purely physiological side my results have been published.'

MacPhee nodded.

'But what has not yet been published,' continued Orfieu, 'is the proof that the Z substance is the organ of memory and prevision. And starting from that, I have been able to construct my chronoscope.'

He turned round and indicated an object which had, of course, engaged no small part of our attention ever since we first entered the room. Its most obvious feature was a white sheet about four feet square stretched on a framework of canes as if for a magic-lantern performance. On a table immediately before it stood a battery with a bulb. Higher than the bulb, and between it and the sheet, there hung a small bunch or tangle of some diaphanous material, arranged into a complicated pattern of folds and convolutions, rather reminiscent of the shapes that a mouthful of tobacco smoke assumes in still air. He gave us to understand that this was the chronoscope proper. It was only about the size of a man's fist.

'I turn on the light, so,' said Orfieu, and the bulb began to shine palely in the surrounding daylight. But he switched it off again at once and continued. 'The rays pass through the chronoscope on to the reflector and our picture of the other time then appears on the sheet.'

There was a pause of a few seconds and then MacPhee said, 'Come on, man. Are you not going to show us any pictures?'

Orfieu was hesitating, but Scudamour, who had risen, came to our aid.

'I think we might show them something right away,' he suggested, 'provided we warn them not to be disappointed. You see,' he added, turning to us, 'the trouble is that in the alien time which we've succeeded in striking the days and nights don't synchronize with ours. It's now six o'clock with us. But *there*, or *then*, or whatever you like to call it, it is only about an hour after midnight, so that you will see hardly anything. It's a great nuisance to us because it means that all our real observation has to be done at night.'

I think that all of us, even MacPhee, were a bit excited by now, and we urged Orfieu to go on with his demonstration.

'Will you have the room darkened or not?' he asked. 'If you don't, you'll see even less. If you do, of course, anyone will be able to say afterwards that Scudamour and I were up to some tricks.'

There was an embarrassed silence.

'You'll understand, Orfieu,' said MacPhee, 'that there's no *personal* imputation — '

'All right, all right,' said Orfieu with a smile. 'Ransom, you won't be able to see there, you'd better come to the sofa. Now, have you all got a clear view of the screen?'

2

Except for a faint buzzing there was complete silence in the room for some moments, so that noises from without became noticeable and the memory of that first glimpse through the chronoscope is for ever associated in my mind with the distant roar of traffic from beyond the river and the voice of a newsboy, much nearer, crying the evening paper. It is strange that we were not more disappointed, for what appeared on the screen was not in itself impressive. It darkened a little in the centre, and above the darkness there came the faint suggestion of some round object slightly more luminous than the surrounding whiteness of the sheet. That was all; but it took us, I think, nearly ten minutes to get tired of it. Then MacPhee gave in.

'You can darken your room, Orfieu,' he grunted.

Scudamour instantly rose. We heard the curtain-rings rattle on the rods; the curtains were heavy and close-fitting; the room vanished and we became invisible to one another. The only light was now the light that flowed from the screen.

The reader must understand at once that it was not like looking at a cinema screen. It was far more real than that. A window seemed to be opened before us, through which we saw the full moon and a few stars; lower down, the mass of some large building. There was a square tower in the building and on one side of this the moonlight shone. I think we made out the billowy shape of trees; then a cloud passed across the moon and for a few moments we were in utter blackness. No one spoke. The cloud passed on, driven by night wind, and the moon shone out again, so bright that some of the objects in the room became visible. It was so real that I expected to hear the noise of the wind in the trees and almost imagined that the temperature had fallen. The cheerful, unimpressed voice of Scudamour broke in upon the awe which was beginning to creep over me.

'There'll be nothing more to see for hours,' he said. 'They're all asleep there.'

But no one suggested that we should pull the curtains and return to daylight.

'Do you know *when* it is?' asked Ransom.

'We can't find out,' replied Orfieu.

'You'll observe,' said MacPhee, 'that in terms of astronomical time it can't be very far away. The moon's just the same, and so are the trees, from what we can see of them.'

'*Where* is it?' I asked.

'Well, that's very difficult,' said Orfieu. 'In daylight it looks as if it ought to be in our own latitude. And theoretically the chronoscope should give us a different time in the very same place – I mean the place the observer is in. But then the days and nights don't coincide with ours.'

'They're not longer, are they?' asked MacPhee suddenly.

'No, they're the same. It's 2 a.m., about, in *their* time, which means that noon for them will come about 4 a.m. tomorrow morning.'

'Do you know what time of the year it is there?'

'Early autumn.'

And all the while the clouds kept moving over the face of the moon and parting to reveal the towered building. I do not think that any revelation of some distant place, not even a peep at the landscape of the planets that wheel round Sirius, could have awakened in me quite such a spectral sense of distance as the slow, harmless progress of that windy night, passing we knew not when.

'Is it in the future or the past?' I queried.

'It is in no period known to archaeology,' said Orfieu. Again we were silent and watched.

'Have you any control over its direction – I mean, its direction in space?' asked MacPhee.

'I think you'd better answer that one, Scudamour,' said Orfieu. 'You've really had much more practice with the thing by now than I have.'

'Well,' said Scudamour, 'it's not very easy to explain. If you try to twiddle the screen round so as to try to get a bit of the landscape, say, to the left of the Dark Tower –'

'The what?' said Ransom.

'Oh – Orfieu and I call this big building the Dark Tower – out of Browning, you know. You see, he and I have had to talk about these things a good deal and it's convenient to have names. Well, if you tried to see what was further to the left by turning the whole thing round, you wouldn't succeed. The picture just slides off the screen and you get nothing. On the other hand, the view does change of itself every now and then, following what Orfieu and I call "interest lines". That is to say, it will follow a single person up the stairs and into the Dark Tower – or a ship along a river. Once it followed a thunderstorm for miles.'

'*Whose* interest does it follow?' asked MacPhee, but no one answered this because Ransom at the same moment said, 'You mention people. What sort of people are they?'

'No, no,' said MacPhee. 'Don't let them start describing. We want our observations to be perfectly independent.'

'Quite right,' said Orfieu.

'You say it follows a man into the Dark Tower,' said I. 'You mean, do you, it follows him till he disappears inside?'

'No,' said Scudamour. 'It sees through walls and things. I know that sounds rather startling, but you must remember this is an external or artificial memory and prevision – as the lens is an external eye. It behaves just like memory – moving from place to place and sometimes jumping, in obedience to laws we don't yet know.'

'But all roughly in the same place,' added Orfieu. 'We don't often get more than ten miles away from the Dark Tower.'

'That's not very like memory,' said I.

'Well, no,' said Orfieu; and silence fell. The wind seemed to be blowing up for a storm in the land we were looking at. The clouds followed one another in ever swifter succession across the face of the moon, and on the right of the picture the waving of the trees became distinctly noticeable. Finally, heavy banks of cloud came up, the whole scene disappeared into a monochrome of dark grey, and Scudamour switched off the light and drew the curtains. We blinked in the sudden inrush of daylight and there was a general shifting of positions and intaking of breath, as among men whose attention has been strained.

'Quarter to seven,' said Orfieu. 'We'd better think about getting ready for dinner. Everyone except old Knellie is down for the vac., so we ought to be able to get away fairly soon afterwards.'

During the whole of our stay in College with Orfieu, his aged colleague Knellie (Cyril Knellie, the now almost forgotten author of *Erotici Graeci Minimi, Table-talk of a Famous Florentine Courtesan* and *Lesbos: A Masque*) was a great trial to us. It would not be fair to mention him in a story about Cambridge without adding that Oxford had produced Knellie and indeed nurtured him till his fortieth year. He was now a shrunk, pale man with a white moustache and a skin like satin that had been badly creased; very carefully dressed; nice in his eating; a little exotic

28

in gesture; and very anxious to be regarded as a man of the world. He was the affectionate type of bore, and I was his selected victim. On the strength of having been at my old college – some time in the nineties – he addressed me as Lu-Lu, a sobriquet I particularly dislike. When dinner was over and Orfieu was just beginning to make his apologies to the old man for withdrawing us on the ground of urgent work, he held up his forefinger as prettily as if he had newly learned the trick.

'No, Orfieu,' he said. 'No. I've promised poor Lu-Lu some of the *real* claret, and I'm not going to let you take him away now.'

'Oh, don't bother about me,' said I hastily.

[Here folio 11 of the manuscript – about 475 words – is missing.]

any words of mine could describe.

Drunk with fatigue, and perhaps a little drunk with claret too, Ransom and I emerged into the open air. Orfieu's rooms lay on the far side of the court. The starlight, and the sweet summer coolness, sobered our mood. We realized afresh that behind certain windows, not fifty yards away, humanity was opening a door that had been sealed from the beginning, and that a train of consequences incalculable for good or evil was on foot.

'What do you think of it all?' I asked.

'I don't like it,' said Ransom. After a short pause he added, 'But I can tell you one thing. I've seen that building – what Scudamour calls the Dark Tower – before.'

'You don't believe in reincarnation?'

'Of course not. I'm a Christian.'

I thought for a minute. 'If it's in the past,' I said, 'then, on Orfieu's theory, there's no reason why lots of people shouldn't "remember" the Dark Tower.'

By this time we had reached Orfieu's staircase.

I suppose that our experience at the moment of entering the room must have been rather like that of entering a cinema; there would have been the same general darkness, the lighted screen, and the groping for unoccupied seats. But it would have been unlike a cinema because of the ghostly silence in which the 'picture' proceeded. All this, however, I can only conjecture in the light of later experiences with the chronoscope; I remember nothing of our entry on this particular evening. What followed has effaced it, for destiny chose this night to pitchfork us brutally, and with no gentle gradations, into something so shocking that, if I had not had the business of recording it always before my mind, it would by now perhaps have been dropped out of my consciousness altogether.

I am going to tell you what we saw in the order which will make it clearest, not in the order which my attention actually followed. At first I had no eyes except for the Man; but here, the room in which he sat will be described first.

We were looking at a chamber of greyish-brown stone which seemed to be lit by morning daylight from windows that were not in our field of vision. The room was about the width of the screen so that we could see the walls on each side as well as the wall that faced us, and each of these three walls was covered down to the floor with decorations in low relief. There was not so much plain surface as you could lay the point of a penknife on. I think it was this intense crowding of ornament that chiefly produced the disagreeable effect of the place, for I do not recall anything specially grotesque or obscene in any single figure. But no figure was single. You would get a floral pattern, but the individual flowers were repeated till the mind reeled. Above that there might be a battle-piece, and the soldiers were as numerous as those of a real army; and above that a fleet, whose sails could not be counted, riding on a sea in which wave rose behind wave for ever and each wave was done in the same relentless detail, up to where at last a regiment of beetles appeared to be marching down to the coast, every beetle distinct, the very joints in their armour traced with an entomologist's accuracy. Whatever one looked at one was aware of more, and still more, to the left of it and the right of it, above it and below it, all equally laborious, reiterative, microscopic, and all equally clamorous for an attention which one could not hope to give and yet had difficulty in withholding. As a result, the whole place seemed to be bursting, I cannot say with life (the word is too sweet), but with some obscure kind of fertility. It was extraordinarily disquieting.

About four feet from the front a high step ran right across the room so that the further part of it formed a kind of dais, and in the side walls at each end of the dais there were doors. One half of this dais — that on our left — was protected by a kind of half-wall or balustrade, which rose about four feet from the surface of the dais and five feet from the lower, and nearer, part of the floor. It came out to the middle of the room and there stopped, leaving the rest of the dais visible. The chair in which the Man was seated was placed on the lower floor in front of the balustrade. He was therefore invisible to anyone who should walk into the room along the dais from the door on the left.

Against the right-hand wall, well forward and opposite the Man, there was a squat pillar surmounted by a curious idol. At first I could hardly make out what it was, but I know it well enough now. It is an image in which a number of small human bodies culminate in a single large head. The bodies are nude, some male and some female. They are very nasty. I do not think they are meant wantonly, unless the taste of the Othertime in such matters differs remarkably from our own. They seem rather to express a savagely satiric vision, as if the sculptor hated and despised what he was making. At any rate, for whatever reason, shrivelled or bloated forms predominate, and there is a free treatment both of morbid anatomy and of senile sexual characteristics.

Then on top there is a huge head — the communal head of all those figures. After full discussion with my colleagues I have decided not to attempt a description of the face. If it were not recognizable (and it is difficult to convey the effect of a face in words), it would be useless; on the other hand, if many readers, especially of the less balanced sort, recognized the face, the results might be disastrous. For at this point I must make a certain statement although the reader will not be able to understand it till he has read further into the book. It is this: that the many-bodied idol is still there in that room. The word 'still' is in some ways misleading, but I cannot help it. The point I want to make is that the things I am describing are not over and done with.

All this description of the room I believe to be necessary. MacPhee, who is beside me as I write, says that I am lengthening it out simply in order to postpone the moment of describing the Man. And he may be right. I freely admit that the memory from which I write is an extremely disagreeable one and that it struggles in the most obstinate manner not to be set down in words.

Yet in the general appearance of the Man there was nothing to shock one. The worst you can say of his face is that it was, by our standards, singularly unattractive. He had a yellowish complexion, but not more so than many Asiatics, and he had lips at once thick and flat like those of a carved Assyrian king. The face looked out from a mass of black hair and beard. But the word 'black' is inadequate. The stiff heavy masses – again reminiscent of carving – could not have been attained in our race without the use of oil, and hair so black would, among us, be lustrous. But this hair showed neither natural lustre nor the gleam of oil. It was dead black, like the darkness in a coal-cellar, a mere negation of colour; and so were the heavy robes in which the Man was swathed down to the feet.

He sat perfectly still. After seeing him, I think I shall never describe anyone in our own time as 'perfectly still' again. His stillness was not like that of a man asleep, nor like that of an artist's model: it was the stillness of a corpse. And oddly enough, it had the curious effect of making one think that it must have begun suddenly – as if something had come down like the blade of a guillotine and cut short the Man's whole history at a moment. But for what followed, we should have thought that he was dead or that he was a waxwork. His eyes were open, but the face had no expression, or none that we could interpret.

MacPhee says that I am again drawing out my description needlessly; going round and round while the most important thing about the Man remains to be described. And he's right. The anatomical absurdity – the incredible thing – how can I write it down in cold blood? Perhaps you, reader, will laugh. We did not, neither then, nor since, in our dreams.

The Man had a sting.

It was in his forehead, like a unicorn's horn. The flesh of the forehead was humped and puckered in the middle, just below the hair, and out of it stuck the sting. It was not very big. It was broad at the base and narrowed quickly to its point, so that its total shape was rather that of a thorn on a rose-branch, or a little pyramid, or a 'man' in the game of halma. It was hard and horny, but not like bone. It was red, like most of the things in a man, and apparently lubricated by some kind of saliva. That is how MacPhee tells me I ought to describe it. But none of us would have dreamed of saying 'lubricated' or 'salivation' at the time: we all thought what Ransom thought – and said:

'Dripping with poison. The brute – the dirty, dirty brute.'

'Has this appeared before?' I asked Orfieu.

'Over and over again,' he answered in a low voice.

'Where is it?'

'Inside the Dark Tower.'

'Hush!' said MacPhee suddenly.

Unless you had sat with us in the dark room and seen the Stingingman, you could hardly imagine with what relief, with what shiftings in our chairs and releases of breath, we saw that the door on the left of the Othertime room had opened and that a young man had entered on the dais. Nor will you understand how we loved that young man. More than one of us confessed afterwards that we had felt an irrational impulse to warn him of the horror sitting silent in the chair – to call out as if our voices could have reached him across whatever unknown centuries lay between us and the Dark Tower.

The young man was concealed from the waist downwards by the balustrade; what was visible of him was naked. He was a fine muscular fellow, bronzed from the open air, and he walked slowly, looking straight before him. His face was not very intelligent, but it had an open and agreeable expression, sobered, apparently, by something like religious awe. So he appears, at least, when I try to analyse my memory: at that moment he appeared to me like an angel.

'What's the matter?' said MacPhee to Orfieu, who had suddenly risen.

'I've seen this done before,' he replied curtly. 'I'm going out to take a turn in the open air.'

'I think I'll come with you,' said Scudamour, and both of them left the room. We did not understand this at the time.

While these words were being spoken, the young man had already advanced to the open part of the dais and stepped down on to the lower floor. We now saw that he was barefoot and dressed only in a sort of kilt. He was obviously engaged in some ritual act. Never looking behind him, he stood motionless for a moment with his gaze fixed on the idol. Then he bowed to it. Then, when he had straightened himself, he took three paces backwards. This brought him to a position in which his calves almost touched the knees of the Stingingman. The latter sat still as ever and his expression did not change; indeed neither of them gave any sign that he was aware of the other's presence. We saw the young man's lips moving as if he were repeating a prayer.

Then, with a movement as much too swift, as his previous immobility had been too still, for humanity – with a movement like the dart of a dragonfly – the Stingingman had shot out his hands and gripped the other by the elbows; and at the same time he put down his head. I suppose it was the sting which made this movement seem so grotesquely animal; the creature was so obviously not letting his head sink in thought as a man might; he was putting

34

it into position like a goat that means to butt.

A frightful convulsion had passed through the victim's body when he first felt himself seized; and as the point of the sting entered his back we saw him writhe in torture, and the sweat gleamed on his suddenly whitened face. The Man had stung him apparently in the spine, pressing in the needle-point of the sting, neither quickly nor slowly, with a surgeon's accuracy. The struggles of his victim did not last long; his limbs relaxed and he hung limp in the grip of the operator. I thought he had been stung to death. But little by little, as we watched, life came back to him – but a different life. He was standing on his own legs again now, no longer hanging, but his stance was stiff. His eyes were staringly open and his face wore a fixed grin. The Stingingman released him. Without once looking behind him, he hopped back on to the dais. Strutting with sharp, jerky movements, lifting his feet unnecessarily high and swinging his arms as if in time to the blaring swagger of some abominable march, he continued his walk along the dais and finally left the room by the door upon our right.

Almost at the same moment the door on the left opened and another young man came in.

In order to avoid telling over and over again what I hope, when once this book is finished, to efface for ever from my memory, I may as well say here and now that I saw this process carried out about two hundred times during our experiments with the chronoscope. The effect on the victims was always the same. They entered the room as men, or (more rarely) women; they left it automata. In recompense – if you call it a recompense – they entered it in awe, and left it all with the same clockwork swagger. The Stingingman displayed neither cruelty nor pity. He sat still, seized, stung, and sat still again with the passionless precision of an insect or a machine.

At this session we saw only four men poisoned: after that we saw another thing which I am afraid must be told. About twenty minutes after his last patient had left the room, the Stingingman rose from his chair and came forward – came to what we could not help regarding as the front of the stage. We now saw him full-face for the first time; and there he stood and stared.

'Great Scot,' said Ransom suddenly. 'Does he see us?'

'It can't be, it can't be,' said MacPhee. 'He must be looking into the other part of that room – the part we can't see.'

And yet the Stingingman slowly moved his eyes, exactly as if he were taking stock of the three of us one by one.

'Why the hell doesn't Orfieu come back?' said I, and realized that I was shouting. My nerves were badly jangled.

And still the Stingingman went on looking at us, as it seemed, or looking at people in his own world who for some reason occupied just the same places in relation to him as we did. It lasted, I suppose, ten minutes or so. What followed must be described briefly and vaguely. He – or it – began to perform a series of acts and gestures so obscene that, even after the experiences we had already had, I could hardly believe my eyes. If you had seen a mentally deficient street-urchin doing the same things at the back of a warehouse in Liverpool docks, with a grin on his face, you would have shuddered. But the peculiar horror of the Stingingman was that he did them with perfect gravity and ritual solemnity and all the time he looked, or seemed to look, unblinkingly at us.

Suddenly the whole scene vanished and we saw once more the exterior of the Dark Tower, the blue sky behind it, and white clouds.

3

Next day, as we sat in the fellows' garden, we arranged our programme. We were languid from insufficient sleep and from the sweetness of late summer all about us. Bees murmured in the foxgloves and a kitten, which had placed itself unasked on Ransom's knees, stretched out its paws in a vain effort to catch, or touch, the smoke of his cigarette. We drew up a time-table according to which we were to take our turns as observers at the chronoscope. I forget the details, for those of us who were off duty so frequently dropped in to share the watch, or else were called up to see some specially interesting phenomenon, that the whole of that fortnight is confused in my mind. College was so empty that Orfieu had been able to find bedrooms for us all on his own staircase. The whole thing, except the scenes on the chronoscope itself, comes back to me as a vague chaos of midnight calls and noonday breakfasts, of sandwiches in the small hours, baths and shaves at unaccustomed times, and always, as a background, that garden which, whether by starlight or sunlight, so often seemed our only link with sanity.

'Well,' said Orfieu, as he finished reading out the corrected time-table, 'that's settled. And there's really no reason why you shouldn't take a couple of days off at the end of next week, Scudamour.'

'Going away?' said I.

'No,' said Scudamour. 'My fiancée is coming down – of course I could put her off till October.'

'Not at all, man, not at all,' said MacPhee. 'If you've been watching those devils all this term, you'll want a change. Send him away for the weekend, Orfieu.'

Orfieu nodded and then smiled. 'You don't like them?' he queried.

'Likes and dislikes ought not to be brought into science, I confess,' said MacPhee; and then after a pause, 'Man, I wish we knew whether it's in the future or the past. But it can't be the past. There'd be bound to be some traces of that civilization left. And if it's the future – God, to think of the world coming to *that,* and that nothing we can do will prevent it.'

'I don't believe,' said I, 'that archaeologists know half so much as you make out. It is only by chance, after all, that pots and skulls get left behind for them to dig up. There may have been dozens of civilizations that have left no trace.'

'What do you think, Ransom?' said Orfieu.

Ransom was sitting with his eyes cast down as he played with the kitten. He was very pale and did not look up as he replied.

'If you want the truth, I'm afraid the things we were looking at last night may be in the future for any of us.' Then, seeing that we did not understand, he added with visible reluctance, 'I think that Dark Tower is in hell.'

The remark might have passed, at least with some of us, for a harmless eccentricity, but I suppose that the experiences of the preceding night had left us in a slightly abnormal condition. For my own part, I remember feeling at that moment – and it has proved an unforgettable moment – an intense anger against Ransom combined with an uprush of wildly unusual and archaic thoughts; thoughts without a name, and sensations which seemed to rise from a remote, almost a pre-natal, past. Orfieu said nothing, but knocked out his pipe on the frame of his deck-chair so violently that it broke, and then flung the fragments away with a curse. MacPhee gave one of his guttural growls and shrugged his shoulders. Even Scudamour looked down his nose as if something indecent had been done, and began to hum a tune. There was rank hatred in the air. Ransom continued to stroke the kitten.

'Mind you,' said MacPhee presently, 'I'm not admitting that those things are in the past or future at all. The whole business may be a hallucination.'

'You are at liberty to make any investigations you like,' said Orfieu with what appeared to me such unnecessary rudeness that I said (much louder than I meant), 'Nobody's talking about investigations. He said a hallucination, not a trick.'

'It was not we who first insisted on having the room darkened, sir,' said Scudamour to me with icy politeness.

'What on earth are you suggesting?' I asked.

'It is you who are making suggestions, sir.'

'I'm doing nothing of the sort.'

'What the devil is the matter with you both?' said Mac-

Phee. 'You're like a pack of children today.'

'It was Mr Lewis who first used the word "trick",' said Scudamour.

MacPhee was about to reply when Ransom suddenly remarked with a smile, 'I'm sorry.' Then, quietly setting down the kitten, he rose and walked away. The device worked admirably. The remaining four of us at once fell to discussing Ransom's peculiarities and in a few minutes we had once more talked ourselves into good humour.

A continuous narrative of our lives and observations from this point to the night on which our real adventures began would serve no purpose. I shall content myself with recording two or three things that now seem of importance.

In the first place, we became familiar with the outside of the Dark Tower by daylight. We learned – what night had concealed during my first view of it – that the building was incomplete. The scaffolding was still up and gangs of labourers were busily employed upon it from sunrise to sunset. They were all of the same type as the young man whom I had seen automatized by the Stingingman, and like him wore no clothing but a short kilt of some red material. I have never seen more energetic workers. They seemed to rush at their task like ants and the rapid complexity of their moving crowds was the most noticeable feature of the whole scene. The background of their activities was the flat, well-timbered country about the Dark Tower; there were no other buildings in sight.

But the workers were not the only characters in the scene. Every now and then it would be invaded by what seemed to be soldiers or police – strutting and grinning columns of men whose clockwork movements made it clear that they had undergone the stinging operation. At least they behaved just as the young worker had behaved after the sting, and we inferred that their behaviour had the same cause. Besides the marching columns, there were invariably a few small pickets of these 'Jerkies' as we called them, posted here and there, apparently to superintend the work. The midday meal for the workmen was brought by a

company of female Jerkies. Every column had its flags and
its band, and even the small pickets usually boasted some
instrument of music. To us, of course, the whole Othertime
world was absolutely silent: in reality, what between the
bands and the noise of the workmen, it must have been
dinning with sound. The pickets carried whips but I never
saw them strike the workmen. Indeed the Jerkies seemed
to be popular and the arrival of one of their larger com-
panies was usually greeted with a short cessation of work
and with gestures that suggested cheering.

I cannot remember how often we had studied this scene
before we began to notice the man whom we called 'Scudamour's double'. It was MacPhee who gave him that name.
Two men, near the front of our field of vision, were engaged
in sawing a block of stone, and I think all of us had been
puzzled for some time by something indefinably familiar
in the face of one of them, when the Scotsman suddenly
cried out, 'It's your double, Scudamour. Look at it, man.
It's your double.'

Once the thing had been stated there was no denying it.
One of the workmen was more than like Scudamour: he
was Scudamour, nail for nail, hair for hair, and the very
expression of his face as he looked up to make a remark
to the other sawyer was one we had all seen on
Scudamour's face a dozen times that very morning. One
or two of us tried to treat the thing as a joke, but I think
Scudamour himself was uncomfortable about it from the
very beginning. It had, however, the advantage of making
these busy scenes (which often occupied the chronoscope for
hours at a time) more interesting. To pick out the Double
in the crowd and follow him wherever he went became our
amusement; and when anyone returned to our sessions after
an absence, his first question was usually 'How's the Double
been getting on?'

Every now and then the scene changed, just as it changes
in imagination. We never discovered why. Without any
power of resistance we would suddenly find ourselves back
in the chamber of the Stingingman, and thence be whisked

away to barrack-like rooms where we saw Jerkies eating, or perhaps to some little cell-like cubicle where a tired work-man lay asleep, and out again to the clouds and the tree-tops. Often we looked for hours at things which repetition had already staled, and were tantalized with hurried glimpses of what was new and interesting.

And all this time none of us doubted that we were look-ing either at the far future or the far past, though MacPhee sometimes felt it his duty to point out that this was not yet proved. And still none of us had noticed the most obvious thing about the scenes we were looking at.

For this discovery we were indebted to MacPhee; but before it can be told there is one more scene to be recorded. As far as I am concerned it began with my looking into the 'observatory', as we now called Orfieu's smaller sitting-room, before I went to bed at about five o'clock one morn-ing. Scudamour was on duty there and I asked him as usual how the Double was getting on.

'I think he's dying,' said Scudamour.

I glanced at the screen and saw at once what he had meant. Everything was very dark but by the light of a single taper I could see that we had before us the interior of one of the small cells in the Dark Tower. There was little more in it than a low bed and a table. On the bed there sat a naked man who was bowing his head till it almost touched his knees and at the same time pressing both his hands to his forehead. As I looked he suddenly straightened himself like one in whom a period of dogged endurance has given way to intolerable pain. He rose and looked wildly about him; his face was white and drawn with suffering but I recognized him as the Double. He took two or three turns about the room and presently stopped at the table to drink greedily from a jug that stood there. Then he turned and groped at the back of his bed. He found a rag there, dipped it in the jug, and pressed it, dripping with water, against his forehead. He repeated the process several times but apparently without gaining relief, for he finally flung the rag from him with a gesture of impatience and stretched himself on the bed. A moment later he was doubled up again, clasping his forehead, and rolling to and fro, while his shoulders shook as if he sobbed.

'Has this been going on long?' I asked.

'Yes, a long time.'

There was a pause.

'The poor devil,' Scudamour broke out. 'Why can't they do something for him? Why doesn't he go and get help? Leave him like that – what a filthy time that Othertime is.'

It was certainly extremely painful to have to watch a fellow creature, however many centuries remote, suffering like that, and to be unable to do, or even to say, anything for his comfort. It was all so real, so like something happening in the same room, that we both felt a certain guilt in being merely passive spectators. At the same time the unusual energy of Scudamour's voice – even a hint of hysteria in it – surprised me. I dropped into the chair beside him.

'I wish to God we'd never started this infernal chronoscope,' he said presently.

'Well,' said I, 'I expect you and Orfieu have had about enough of it.'

'Enough – !'

'Look here, you mustn't let it get on your nerves. As we can't do anything for that poor fellow, I can't see that there's any point in watching him all night.'

'The moment I knocked off the scene might change.'

'Well, I'll stay. I'm not particularly sleepy.'

'Nor am I. And there's nothing wrong with my nerves, only I've got such a splitting headache. Thanks all the same.'

'Well, if you've a headache you'd certainly better knock off.'

'It isn't exactly the headache . . . it's nothing to make a fuss about. Not really. But it's just here.'

He forgot that in the darkness I could not see his gesture; for all this time we could not see each other, but only (and that by the light of a taper burning in another world) the Double, shut up alone with his pain in some cell of the

Dark Tower. Yet I hardly needed Scudamour's next words.

'It's just where *his* is,' he whispered. 'Here in my fore-head. Like his. I've got *his* pain, not my own. You don't think—'

What both of us thought was hardly capable of being put into words. What I actually said was, 'I think if we allow our imaginations to run away with us over this chronoscope, we'll go off our heads. We're all dead tired, you most of all, and we've seen enough of the Othertime to show that D.T. is a game in comparison. It's no wonder you've got a bad head. Now look here. With the curtains drawn we can see just enough of what's going on on the screen to notice whether it shifts to somewhere else.' I got up and pulled back the curtains, and the blessed daylight and the noise of the birds came pouring in. 'Now,' I continued, 'go and get some aspirin and make a pot of strong tea for the pair of us and let's sit it out together and be comfortable.'

It was hours later, when the room had been darkened again and Scudamour and I were both (fortunately) in bed, that dawn came into the Double's room in Othertime. What it revealed I learned from Ransom. He said that the taper had apparently burned itself out, and that when there was enough daylight to see things by, they found the bed empty. It took them some time to discover the Double; when at last they made him out, he was sitting on the floor in one corner all hunched up. He was not now writhing or showing any signs of pain—indeed he was unnaturally still and stiff. His face was in shadow. He sat like that for a long time while the room grew lighter and nothing happened. At last the light fell on his face. At first they thought he had a bruise on his forehead and then they thought he had a wound. The reader will understand that they began with the knowledge that he had passed the night in great pain, and that is doubtless why they did not guess the truth sooner. They did not guess it until a Jerky had come into the room swaggering and cracking his whip, and then, after a glance at the Double, had fallen flat on his face. He went out backwards covering his eyes with his hands. Other Jerkies, and some workmen, came in. They also fell flat and went out backwards. At last female Jerkies came in. They crawled on their bellies, dragging a black robe, and laid it on the bed, and crawled out again. A number of people, all flat on their faces, waited just inside the door of the cell. The Double had watched all this without moving. Now he rose and came into the centre of the room (his worshippers grovelled closer to the floor and Ransom says they did not kiss, but licked, it) and the truth became visible to our observers. He had grown a sting. The pains of the night had been birth pains. His face was still recognizable as that of Scudamour's double, but it had already the yellow pallor and immobility of the man we had seen in the carved room. When he had put on the black robe he was unmistakable: he had gone to bed a man and risen a Stingingman.

Of course this could not be concealed from Scudamour and, equally of course, it did not help to ease the nervous tension in which he was living. We all of us agreed afterwards that from this time on he was increasingly strange in his behaviour; and even at the time Ransom urged Orfieu to persuade him to give up his work immediately and not to wait for his fiancée's visit. I remember Ransom saying, 'That young fellow may blow up any moment.' We ought all to have taken more notice of this. In our defence I may plead that Miss Bembridge was expected in a very few days (three, I think), that we were very much preoccupied with our observations, and that what happened on the following day was startling enough to drive all other considerations out of our heads.

It was MacPhee who released the bomb. We were all together in the observatory, watching the usual busy scene outside the Dark Tower – and watching it inattentively because it was so usual – when he suddenly swore and then stood up.

'Orfieu!' he said.

All our heads turned in MacPhee's direction. His voice

44

had not sounded exactly angry, but it had a note of solemn adjuration in it that was more compelling than anger.

'Orfieu,' he said again, 'once and for all. What game are you playing with us?'

'I don't know what you mean,' said Orfieu.

'Understand,' said MacPhee, 'I'm not going to quarrel with you. But I'm a busy man. If all this has been a hoax, I'll not call you a humbug – you can have your joke – but I'm not going to stay here to be hoaxed any longer.'

'A hoax?'

'Aye. I didn't say a trick, so you need not get angry. I said a hoax. But I'm asking you now, on your word and honour – is it a hoax?'

'No, it isn't. What on earth do you mean?'

MacPhee stared at him for a moment almost, I think, in the hope of detecting some sign of embarrassment in his face; but there was none. Then, plunging his hands into his pockets, the Scotsman began pacing to and fro with an air of desperation.

'Very well,' he said. 'Very well. But if it's not a hoax, we're all madmen. The universe is mad. And we're blind as bats too.' He suddenly paused in his stride and wheeled round to address the whole company. 'Do you mean to tell me that not one of you recognizes that building?' – here he flung out a hand towards the Dark Tower.

'Yes,' said Ransom, 'I thought it familiar from the very first, but I can't put a name to it.'

'Then you're less of a fool than the rest of us,' said Mac-Phee. 'You're the one-eyed man among the blind.' He stared at us again as if awaiting some response.

'Well,' said Orfieu at last, 'how should we recognize it?'

'Why, man,' said MacPhee, 'you've seen it hundreds of times. You could see it from here if the curtains were drawn.' He walked to the window and pulled them. We all came crowding behind him to look out, but after a glance he turned back into the room. 'I'm wrong,' he said. 'The houses get in the way.'

I was beginning to wonder whether MacPhee were out

45

of his wits, when Scudamour said, 'You don't mean – ?' and paused.

'Go on,' said MacPhee.

'It's too fantastic,' said Scudamour, and at the same moment Orfieu suddenly said, 'I've got it.'

'So have I,' said Ransom. 'The Dark Tower is an almost exact replica of the new university library here in Cambridge.'

There was complete silence for several seconds.

Orfieu was the first who attempted to pick up the fragments of our previous tranquillity and see if they could be fitted together again.

'There certainly is a resemblance,' he began, 'a distinct resemblance. I'm glad you have pointed it out. But whether – '

'Resemblance, your grandmother,' said MacPhee. 'They're identical, except that the tower in there' (he pointed to the screen) 'is not quite finished. Here, Lewis, you can draw. Sit down and do us a wee sketch of the Dark Tower.'

I cannot really draw very well, but I did as I was told and succeeded in producing something fairly recognizable. As soon as it was finished we all went out into the town except Ransom, who volunteered to stay behind and watch the chronoscope. It was after one o'clock when we returned, very hungry for our lunch and very thirsty for the tankards of beer which Orfieu provided. Our investigations had taken us a long time because it was not easy to find a place from which we could get the university library at just the same angle as the Dark Tower – and that, by the by, may explain our failure to recognize it at the outset. But when at last we had found the right position MacPhee's theory became irresistible. Orfieu and Scudamour both fought against it as hard as they could – Orfieu coldly, like an *esprit fort,* and Scudamour with a passion which I did not then fully understand. It was almost as if he were begging us not to accept it. In the end, however, the facts were too strong for both of them. The library and the Dark Tower corresponded in every detail, except that one was finished and the other was still in the hands of the builders.

We were so thirsty that we did not think about lunch till we had drunk our pints. Then, having been assured by Orfieu's servant that Mr Knellie had had his lunch and gone out of college, we stole into the cool darkness of the combination room and tackled our bread and cheese.

'Well,' said Orficu, 'this is a most remarkable discovery and you certainly have the laugh of us all, MacPhee. But when one comes to think it over, I don't know why we should be very surprised. It only proves that the time we're looking at is in the future.'

'How do you mean?' said I.

'Well obviously, the Dark Tower is an imitation of the university library. *We* have an imitation of the Colosseum somewhere in Scotland and an imitation of the Bridge of Sighs in Oxford – ghastly things they both are. In the same way, those Othertime people have an imitation of what to them is the ancient British Library at Cambridge. It's not at all odd.'

'I think it is very odd,' said MacPhee.

'But why?' asked Orfieu. 'We have always thought that what we see on the screen is in the same place as ourselves, whatever time it may be. In other words, those people are living – or will be living – on the site of Cambridge. The library has survived for centuries and at last fallen, and now they are putting up a replica. Probably they have some superstition about it. You must remember that to them it would be almost infinitely ancient.'

'That's just the trouble,' said MacPhee. 'Far too ancient. It would have disappeared centuries – millions of centuries, maybe – before their time.'

'How do you know they are so far in the future?' asked Ransom.

'Look at their anatomy. The human body has changed. Unless something very queer occurs to speed up the evolutionary process, it will take nature a good time to produce human heads that can grow stings. It's not a question of

47

centuries – it's a question of millions, or thousands of millions, of years.'

'Nowadays,' said I, 'some people don't seem to agree about evolution being necessarily so very gradual.'

'I know,' said MacPhee. 'But they're wrong. I'm talking of science, not of Butler and Bergson and Shaw and all those whigmaleeries.'

'I don't think Bergson – ', I was beginning, when Scudamour suddenly broke out, 'Oh we may as well chuck it, chuck it, chuck it. What's the good of finding all those explanations why the university library should be in Othertime when they won't explain why I'm there? They've got one of our buildings; and they've got me too, worse luck. They may have hundreds of people in there – people who are now alive – and we haven't recognized them. And that brute, the first Stingingman – the only one till I grew my sting – do you remember how he came to the front and looked at us? Do you still think he didn't see us? Do you still think it's all only in the future? Don't you see, it's all . . . all mixed up with *us* somehow – bits of our world in there, or bits of it out here among us.'

He had been speaking with his eyes on the table, and as he looked up he caught us exchanging glances. This did not mend matters.

'I see I'm making myself unpopular,' he went on, 'just as Dr Ransom did the other day. Well, I dare say I am rather poor company at present. You wait till you see yourselves in Othertime, and we'll find how you like it. Of course I oughtn't to complain. This is science. And who ever heard of a new scientific discovery which didn't show that the real universe was even fouler and meaner and more dangerous than you had supposed? I never went in for religion, but I begin to think Dr Ransom was right. I think we have tapped whatever reality is behind all the old stories about hell and devils and witches. I don't know. Some filthy sort of something going on alongside the ordinary world and all mixed up with it.'

Ransom was able to meet him on this ground with perfect

naturalness and obvious sincerity.

'As a matter of fact, Scudamour,' he said, 'I've changed my mind. I don't think the world we see through the chronoscope is hell, because it seems to contain quite decent, happy people, along with the Jerkies and the Stingingmen.'

'Yes, and the decent people get automatized.'

'I know, and very bad luck it is. But a world in which beastly things can happen to people through no fault of their own – or, at least, not mainly through their own fault – isn't hell: it's only our own world over again. It only has to be faced, like our own world. Even if one was taken there – '

Scudamour shuddered. The rest of us thought Ransom was being very unwise, but I now think he was right. He usually is.

'Even if one was taken in there – which would be worse than merely seeing one's double there – it wouldn't be essentially different from other misfortunes. And misfortune is not hell, not by a long way. A man can't be *taken* to hell, or *sent* to hell: you can only get there on your own steam.'

Scudamour, who had at least paid Ransom the compliment of listening to him with great attention, now asked him, 'And *what* do you think the Othertime is?'

'Well,' said Ransom, 'like you, I am extremely doubtful if it is simply the future. I agree that it is much too mixed up with us for that. And I've been wondering for several days whether the past and the present and the future are the only times that exist.'

'What do you mean?' asked Orfieu.

'I don't know yet,' said Ransom. 'In the meanwhile, have we positive proof that what we are seeing is a time at all?'

'Well,' said Orfieu after a pause, 'I suppose not. Not irrefutable proof. It is, at present, much the easiest hypothesis.'

And that was all that was said at lunch. Two more things happened this day. One was that MacPhee, who had been observing in the afternoon, told me at dinner-time that the

'new Stingingman' or 'Scudamour's double' was now en-
sconced in the carved room. We did not know what had
become of the old Stingingman. Some thought the Double
must have defeated him as a new bull defeats an old bull and
becomes master of the herd. Others imagined he might have
succeeded him peacefully according to the rules of some
sort of diabolical civil service. The whole conception of
Othertime was altering now that we knew there could be
more than one Stingingman. 'A whole stinging caste,' said
MacPhee. 'A centrocracy,' suggested Ransom.

The other event was, in itself, unimportant. Something
went wrong with the college electric light and Orfieu, on
the morning watch, had to use candles.

4

It must have been a Sunday, I think, when the lights failed,
or else all the electricians in Cambridge were engaged – at
any rate, we were still using candles when we assembled in
Orfieu's rooms after dinner. The little lamp in front of the
chronoscope, which worked off its own battery, was of
course unaffected. The curtains were drawn, the candles
blown out, and we found ourselves once more looking at
the carved room – and almost immediately I realized with
a faint sensation of nausea that we were in for another of
the stinging scenes.

This was the first time I had seen the Double since his
transformation, and it was a strange experience. He was
already very like the original Stingingman – in some ways
more like him than he was like Scudamour. He had the
same yellowish pallor and the same immobility; both, indeed,
were more noticeable in him than in his predecessor because
he lacked the beard. At the same time, however, his resemblance to Scudamour was quite undiminished. One sometimes sees this paradox on the faces of the dead. They look
infinitely changed from what they were in life, yet unmis-

takably the same. A resemblance to some distant relation, never before suspected, may creep into the corpse's face, but under that new resemblance the pitiful identity between corpse and man remains. He looks more and more like his grandfather but no less like himself. Something of this sort was happening with the Double. He had not ceased to look like Scudamour : rather, if I may so express it, he looked like Scudamour-looking-like-a-Stingingman. And one result of this was to show the characteristics of the Stingingman face in a new light. The pallor, the expressionless calm, even the horrible frontal deformity itself, now that I saw them induced upon a familiar face, acquired a different horror. I had never thought of pitying the original Stingingman, never suspected that he might be a horror to himself. Now I found that I thought of the poison as pain : of the sting as a solid promontory of anguish bursting out of a tortured head. And then, as the Double put down his head and coolly transfixed his first victim, I felt something like shame. It was as if one had caught Scudamour himself – Scudamour in the grip of madness or of some perversion equivalent to madness – at the moment of performing some monstrous, yet also petty, abomination. I began to have an inkling of how Scudamour himself must feel. Believing him to be at my side, I turned with the vague idea of saying something that might make him feel more comfortable, when to my surprise a quite unexpected voice said, 'Charming. Charming. I had no idea that our age was producing work of this quality.'

It was Knellie. None of us had had any idea that he had followed us into the observatory.

'Oh, it's you, is it ?' said Orfieu.

'I hope I do not intrude, my dear fellow,' said the old man. 'It will be very kind of you, very kind indeed, if you allow me to remain. It is a privilege to be present at the performance of so great a work of art.'

'This is not a cinematograph, you know, Mr Knellie,' said MacPhee.

'I did not for a moment suggest that dreadful name,' said

Knellie in a reverential voice. 'I fully understand that work like this differs *toto caelo* from the vulgarities of the popular theatres. And I understand, too, the reticence – might I say the secrecy? – of your proceedings. You cannot at present show such work to the British philistine. But I am hurt, Orfieu, that you did not take me into your confidence. I trust I, at least, am pretty free from prejudices. Why, my dear fellow, I was preaching the complete moral freedom of the artist when you were a child. May I ask who is the supreme genius to whom we are indebted for this fantasia?'

And while he talked two human beings had come in, had worshipped the idol, been seized and stung, and strutted out again. Scudamour could stand it no longer.

'Do you mean to say you *like* it?' he cried.

'Like it?' said Knellie thoughtfully. 'Does one *like* great art? One responds – perceives – intuits – sympathizes.'

Scudamour had risen. I could not see his face.

'Orfieu,' he said suddenly, 'we must find a way of getting *at* those brutes.'

'You know it's impossible,' said Orfieu. 'We've been into that all before. You can't travel in time. We'd have no bodies *there*.'

'It's not so obvious that *I* shouldn't,' said Scudamour. I had been hoping for some time that this point would not occur to him.

'I am not sure that I understand either of you,' said Knellie, making the assumption that the conversation had been addressed to him with such security that no one could accuse him of interrupting. 'And I don't think time has much to do with it. Surely art is timeless. But who is the artist? Who invented this scene – these superb masses – this splendid, sombre insolence? Who is it *by*?'

'It's by the Devil, if you want to know,' shouted Scudamour.

'Ah –,' said Knellie very slowly, 'I see what you mean. Perhaps in a certain sense that is true of all art at its supreme moments. Didn't poor Oscar say something like that – ?'

'Look out!' cried Scudamour. 'Camilla! For God's sake!'

It took me the fraction of a second to realize that he was shouting not at us but at someone on the screen. And after that everything happened so quickly that I can hardly describe it. I remember seeing a girl – a tall, straight girl with brown hair – coming into the carved room from the left along the dais as dozens of other victims had come in, both men and women. I remember, at the very same moment, a shout from Orfieu (the words were something like 'Don't be a fool!') and the sight of Orfieu rushing forward, like a man about to tackle at football. He was doing this to intercept Scudamour who had suddenly and inexplicably plunged forward, with his head down, straight at the chronoscope. Then, all in an instant, I saw Orfieu reeling back under the impact of the younger and heavier man, I heard the deafening noise of a broken electric light bulb, I felt Knellie's tremulous hands grab me by the sleeve, and found myself sitting on the floor in absolute darkness.

The room was perfectly still for a moment. Then I heard the unmistakable sound of dripping – someone's drink had apparently been overturned. Then came a voice, Mac-Phee's.

'Is anyone hurt?' it said.

'I'm all right,' said Orfieu's voice in the tone of a man who is considerably hurt. 'Got my head a nasty knock, that's all.'

'Are you hurt, Scudamour?' asked MacPhee.

But instead of Scudamour's voice it was Knellie's that replied – in a sort of silvery whine, if a whine can be silvery – 'I'm a good deal shaken. I think if someone could bring me a glass of really good brandy I should be able to get to my own rooms.'

Exclamations of pain burst simultaneously from Orfieu and MacPhee who had struck their heads smartly together in the darkness. The room was full of noises and movements now as we searched for matches. Someone or other was successful. Blinking as the light flared up, I had a momentary vision of a dark figure – presumably Scudamour's –

rising from amidst the wreck of the chronoscope. Then the match went out.

'It's all right,' said MacPhee. 'I've got the box now. Oh damnation –'

'What's wrong?' said I.

'Man, I've opened it upside down and they're all away out on the floor. Wait a bit now, wait a bit. Are you all right, Lewis?'

'Oh yes, I'm all right.'

'And are you all right, Scudamour?'

There was no answer. Then MacPhee found a match and succeeded in lighting a candle. I found myself looking at the face of a stranger. Then, with something of a shock, I realized that it was Scudamour's face. Two things had, I think, prevented me from recognizing him at first. One was the odd way in which he was looking at us. The other was the fact that the candlelight found him engaged in retreating towards the door. 'Retreating' is exactly the word: he was moving backwards as quickly as he could without exciting attention, and at the same time keeping his eyes fixed on us. He was, in fact, behaving exactly like a man of iron nerves suddenly placed among enemies.

'What's the matter with you, Scudamour?' said Orfieu.

But the young man made no reply, and now his hand was on the door handle. The rest of us were still staring at him in bewilderment when Ransom suddenly leaped from his chair. 'Quick! Quick!' he cried. 'Don't let him go,' and with that he flung himself on the retreating figure. The other, who had by this time opened the door, put down his head – the gesture had now a ghastly familiarity for us all – butted Ransom in the stomach, and disappeared.

Ransom was doubled up and could say nothing for some minutes. Knellie was beginning to murmur something about brandy when MacPhee turned to Orfieu and me.

'Are we all mad?' he said. 'What's happening to us? First Scudamour and then Ransom. And where's Scudamour gone to?'

'I don't know,' said Orfieu contemplating the wreck of

the chronoscope, 'and I'm tempted to say I don't care. He's made hay of a year's work, bloody young fool, that's all I know.'

'Why did he go for you like that?'

'He wasn't going for me, he was going for the chronoscope. Trying to jump *through* it, the young ass.'

'To jump into the Othertime, you mean?'

'Yes. Of course you might as well try to jump on to the moon through a telescope.'

'But what set him off?'

'What he saw on the screen.'

'But that's no worse than he's seen dozens of times.'

'Ah, but you don't understand,' said Orfieu. 'It's much worse. That girl who came in – she's another double.'

'What do you mean?'

'It took my breath away. She's as like a certain real woman – I mean, a woman in *our* time – as the old double is like Scudamour. And the woman she is like is Camilla Bembridge.'

The name meant nothing to us. Orfieu sat down with a gesture of impatience. 'I forgot, you wouldn't know,' he said, 'but Camilla Bembridge is the girl he's going to marry.'

MacPhee whistled.

'You can't blame the poor devil, Orfieu,' he said. 'It's enough to loosen a screw in the soundest head. To see a copy of yourself first, and then to see it doing *that* to a copy of your sweetheart . . . I wonder where he's gone.'

By this time Ransom had recovered his speech.

'So do I,' he said. 'I wonder very much. Why on earth did none of you help me to stop him?'

'Why should he be stopped?' said I.

'Come on,' said Ransom, 'don't you see? No, there's not a moment to spare. We'll talk about it afterwards.'

I think MacPhee saw what was in Ransom's mind from the first. I certainly did not, but when I saw the other two leaving the room I followed them. Orfieu remained behind, absorbed, apparently, in investigating the ruin of his chronoscope. Knellie was still nursing his bruise and murmuring about good brandy.

Ransom led us at once to the great gate of the college. It was only about nine o'clock and the light showed in the porter's lodge. As I caught up with the others the porter was just telling Ransom that he had not seen Mr Scudamour go out.

'Is there any other way out of college?' asked Ransom.

'Only the St Patrick gate, sir,' said the porter, 'and it'd be shut in the vacation.'

'Ah – but Mr Scudamour would have a key?'

'Well he ought to have a key,' said the porter. 'But I reckon he's mislaid it, seeing as he borrowed one off me the night before last and gave it back to me yesterday morning. I said to myself at the time, Mr Scudamour's gone and mislaid his key again. Shall I give him any message, sir, if I do see him?'

'Yes,' said MacPhee after a moment's thought. 'Tell him all's well and ask him to go to Dr Orfieu as soon as he can.'

We moved away from the lodge.

'Quick,' said Ransom. 'I'll try his rooms and you two go to the other gate.'

'Come on,' said MacPhee. I wanted to question him but he was running now, and in a few seconds we were at the St Patrick gate. I am not sure what he expected to find there, but he was certainly disappointed.

'What on earth is the matter?' I asked him as he turned away from it. But at the same moment I heard the sound of hasty footsteps and Ransom appeared at the other end of the path.

'His rooms are empty,' he shouted.

'He might be in any of these rooms then?' replied MacPhee, indicating with a wave of his hand the rows of windows which gazed down on the little court with that peculiarly dead expression familiar to all who have lived in a college during the vacation.

'No,' said Ransom. 'Thank heaven they lock them up.'

'Are you never going to tell me,' I began, when suddenly

MacPhee seized my arm and pointed. Ransom had reached us by now : all three of us stood in a bunch together, holding our breaths, and looking up.

The block of buildings which shut off our view towards the west was of a type common in university towns – two storeys of full-sized windows, then a row of battlements, and then dormer-windows behind the battlements projecting from a high-pitched roof. The sky behind it was clear and tinted with the greenish-blue that sometimes follows sunset. Against this, clear as a shape cut out of black paper, a man was moving on the ridge-tiles. He was not crouching, or going on all fours, or even spreading out his arms to balance himself : he was walking with his hands clasped behind his back as easily as I might walk on level ground, and he was turning his head slowly from left to right like one who takes stock of his surroundings.

'That's him, all right,' said MacPhee.

'Mad?' I suggested.

'Oh worse, worse,' replied Ransom, and then, 'Look, he's going down.'

'And on the outside,' added MacPhee.

'Quick,' said Ransom. 'That'll bring him down into Pat's Lane. There's just a chance.'

Once more we dashed back to the great gate, all of us, this time running as fast as we could, for I had seen enough to convince me that Scudamour must be captured at all costs. The porter seemed to move with maddening slowness as he came out of his lodge to open the postern. I felt the seconds ticking past as he fumbled for his key – talking, always talking – and as Ransom and I for very haste impeded each other at the narrow opening, MacPhee behind growled at us to get on. Then we were out at last and racing along the front of the college and round into Pat's Lane – a silent little alley between two colleges, defended from wheeled traffic by a couple of posts. I do not know how far we ran down it : over the bridge, anyway, and far enough to see the buses and cars on a big thoroughfare beyond the river. It is difficult to run seriously when you have no certainty whether your quarry is ahead of you or behind you. We tried several directions. From running we came to quick walking; from quick walking to slow walking; from slow walking to indeterminate hanging about. Finally, at about half past ten, we were all standing still (in Pat's Lane again) mopping our foreheads.

'Poor Scudamour,' I panted. 'But it may be only temporary.'

'Temporary?' said Ransom in a voice that made me pause.

'What's that?' I asked.

'You said "temporary". What hope is there of getting him back? Specially if we've lost the other one?'

'What are you talking about? What other one?'

'The one we've been chasing.'

'You mean Scudamour.'

Ransom gave me a long look. 'That!' he said. 'That wasn't Scudamour.'

I stared at him, not knowing what I thought but knowing that in my thoughts there was something horrible. He went on.

'That wasn't Scudamour who winded me. Did it look like him? Why did it not answer? Why was it backing out of the room? Why did it put down its head and butt? Scudamour wouldn't fight that way if he wanted to fight. Don't you see? When it put down its head it was relying on something it thought it had – something it had been in the habit of using. Namely, a sting.'

'You mean,' said I, resisting a strong feeling of sickness, 'you mean that what we saw on the roof was . . . was the Stingingman?'

'I thought you knew,' said Ransom.

'Then where's the real Scudamour?'

'God help him,' said Ransom. 'If he's alive he's in the Dark Tower in Othertime.'

'Jumped through the chronoscope? – but this is fantastic, Ransom. Didn't Orfieu explain all along that it's only like a telescope? The things we've been seeing weren't really close to us, they were millions of years away.'

'I know that's Orfieu's theory. But what is the evidence for it? And does it explain why Othertime is full of replicas of things in our own world? What do you think, Mac-Phee?'

'I think,' said MacPhee, 'that it is now perfectly certain that he is working with forces he does not understand, and that none of us knows where or when the Othertime world is or how it is related to our own.'

'Except,' said Ransom, 'that it contains these replicas – one building, one man, and one woman so far. There may be any number of others.'

'And what, exactly, do you think has happened?' I asked.

'You remember what Orfieu said the first evening about time-travel being impossible, because you'd have no body in the other time when you got there. Well, isn't it obvious that if you got two times that had replicas that difficulty would be overcome? In other words I think that the Double we saw on the screen had a body not merely like poor Scudamour's but the same: I mean, that the very same matter which made up Scudamour's body in 1938 made up that brute's body in Othertime. Now if that were so – and if you then, by any contrivance, brought the two times into contact, so to speak . . . you see?'

'You mean they might . . . might just jump across?'

'Yes, in a sense. Scudamour, under the influence of a strong emotion, makes what you might call a psychological leap or lunge at the Othertime. Ordinarily nothing would result – or perhaps death. But as bad luck would have it on this occasion, his own body – the very same he's used all his life in *our* time – is there waiting for him. The Other-time occupant of that body is caught off his guard – simply pushed out of his body – but since that identical body is waiting for him in 1938, he inevitably slips into it and finds himself in Cambridge.'

'This is getting very difficult,' said I. 'I'm not sure that I understand about these two bodies.'

'But there aren't *two* bodies. There's only one body exist-ing at two different times – just as that tree existed yesterday and today.'

'What do you think of it, MacPhee?' I asked.

'Well,' said MacPhee, 'I do not start with the simple theory of an entity called the soul as our friend does, and that makes things more complicated for me. But I agree that the behaviour of Scudamour's body, since the crash, is just what we should expect to see if that body had acquired the memory and psychology of the Stingingman. I am therefore ready, as a scientist, to work on Ransom's hypothesis for the present. And I may add that, as a creature of the passions, emotions, and imagination, I don't feel – I'm speaking of *feeling,* ye understand – any doubt about it. What's puzzling me is something else.'

We both turned to him with the same question.

'I'm wondering,' said MacPhee, 'about all these replicas. It's long odds – in fact it's all but infinite odds – against getting the same particles organized as a human body in two different times. And now we've got that happening twice, the boy *and* the girl. And then there's the building. Man, there's too much coincidence about this affair.'

There was silence for a few moments, and then, wrinkling his brow, he proceeded, half to himself, 'I don't know at all. I don't know. But could it be the other way round? Not that we happen to have reached a time that contains replicas of our own, but that it's the replicas that are bringing the times together – a sort of gravitation. You see, if two times contained *exactly* the same distribution of matter, they would become simply the same time ... and if they contained *some* identical distributions they might approach ... I don't know. It's all daft.'

'On that view,' said Ransom, 'the chronoscope would be of quite secondary importance.'

'Ach!' ejaculated MacPhee. 'What's the chronoscope got to do with it? It produces no phenomena, it only lets you see them. This was all going on before Orfieu made his instrument and would have been going on whether or no.'

'What do you mean by "this"?' I asked.

'I hardly know,' said MacPhee after a long pause, 'but

I think we're in for more than Orfieu supposes.'

'In the meantime,' said Ransom, 'we must get back to Orfieu and make some plans. Every minute that creature may be getting further away.'

'He can't do much harm without his sting, I suppose.' said I.

'I shouldn't be too sure even of that,' said Ransom. 'But I was thinking of something else. Don't you see that our only chance of ever getting Scudamour back is to bring him and the Stingingman together *again* – with a chronoscope between them? Once we lose touch with the Stingingman our last hope is gone.'

'In that case,' said I, 'he ought to have the same motive for sticking to us, if he wants to get back to his own time.'

We were now in sight of the college gate and already instinctively turning over in our minds what we would say to Orfieu, when suddenly the postern opened and Orfieu himself appeared – an Orfieu I had not yet seen for he was in a towering rage. He wanted to know where – where the hell – we'd all been and why we'd left him to face the music. We inquired, not in the best of tempers ourselves, what music he meant.

'That infernal woman,' snapped Orfieu. 'Yes, Scudamour's fiancée. The Bembridge woman. On the telephone. And now, what are you going to tell her when she comes round tomorrow?'

5

At this point it will be convenient if my narrative turns to Scudamour. The reader will understand that the rest of us heard his story much later; that we heard it gradually and with all those repetitions and interruptions which arise in conversation. Here, however, it will be straightened out and tidied up for your benefit. No doubt I lose something from the purely literary point of view by not leaving you for the next few chapters in the same uncertainty which we actually endured for the next few weeks, but literature is not here my chief concern.

According to Scudamour's account he had no plan of action in his mind when he rose and leaped upon the chronoscope. Indeed he would never have done so if his excitement had allowed him to reflect, for, like the rest of us, he regarded the instrument as a kind of telescope. He had no belief that you could get through it into Othertime. All he knew was that the sight of Camilla in the clutches of the Stingingman was more than he could bear. He felt that he must smash something – preferably the Stingingman, but at any rate something – or go mad. In other words, he 'saw red'.

He remembers dashing forward with outstretched hands, but he does not remember the sound of the breaking bulb. It seemed to him that as his hands went out he just found them closing on the girl's arms. His impression was one of incredulous triumph : he thought in some confused way that he had pulled Camilla out of Othertime – right through the screen into Orfieu's room. He thinks that he shouted out something like 'It's all right, Camilla. It's me.'

The girl's back was towards him and he was holding her by the elbows. She twisted herself and looked back over her shoulder as he spoke. He still thought that it was Camilla and was not surprised that she was pale and looked terrified. Then he felt her grow suddenly limp in his hands and realized that she was going to faint.

He sprang up at this – for he found that he was sitting – and laid her in his chair, at the same time shouting to the rest of us to help. It was at this moment that he became aware of his novel surroundings. Up to that point there had been a certain strangeness in the whole experience. It had been more like meeting Camilla in a dream than like meeting her in real life; but, like a dream, it was accepted without question. But as he shouted to us a number of facts were forced upon him all at once. In the first place he realized that the language in which he had shouted was not English. Secondly, that the chair in which he was laying the girl (whom he still thought of as Camilla) was not one of the chairs in Orfieu's room – and also that he was not in his ordinary clothes. But what startled him far more was that in the very act of setting the girl down he found his whole mind reeling under the effort of resisting a desire which horrified him both by its content and by its almost maniacal strength. He wanted to sting. There was a cloud of pain in his head so that he felt his head would burst if he did not sting. And for one horrible moment it seemed to him that to sting Camilla would be the most natural thing in the world. For what other purpose was she there?

Of course Scudamour has read his psychoanalysis. He is perfectly well aware that under abnormal conditions a much more natural desire might disguise itself in this grotesque form. But he is pretty sure that this was not what was happening. The pain and pressure in his forehead, as he still remembers them, leave no room for doubt. This was a desire with a real physiological basis. He was full of poison and ached to discharge it.

As soon as he realized what his body was urging him to do he fell back several paces from the chair. He dared not look at the girl for a few minutes, whatever assistance she might need : certainly he must not go near her. As he stood thus, with clenched hands, fighting down the riot of his senses, he took in his surroundings without much immediate attention. He was certainly in the carved room of the Dark Tower. On his right was the dais with the balustrade which he already knew so well. On his left was that part of the room which none of us had ever seen. It was not very large – perhaps about twenty feet long. The walls were completely covered with such decorations as I have described before. There was another door in the far wall and, on each side of this, a low stone seat running the width of the room. But between him and that seat there was something that took his breath away; it was a broken chronoscope.

In all essentials it was identical with Orfieu's instrument. There was a wooden frame from which, at this moment, the shreds of a torn screen were hanging. On a table in front of this there hung a grey convoluted object which he had no difficulty in recognizing. With a sudden gleam of hope he bent to examine it. It was torn in two places and quite useless.

I think it is greatly to Scudamour's credit that he retained his self-control. His own account of the matter is that the terror which arose in his mind was so great that the mind simply refused it and left him comparatively cool and resolute. He realized in an abstract sort of way that he was cut off from all hope of ever regaining our world, surrounded on every side by the unknown, and burdened with a horrible physical deformity from which horrible and, perhaps in the long run, irresistible desires would pour into his consciousness at every moment. But he did not apprehend all this emotionally. That, at least, is what he says. I myself still believe that he showed extraordinary manhood.

By this time the girl had opened her eyes and was staring at him with an expression of terrified wonder. He tried to smile at her, and realized that the muscles of his face — the face he now had — were very unused to smiling.

'It's all right,' he said. 'Don't be afraid. I will not sting you.'

'What is that?' said the girl almost in a whisper. 'What do you mean?'

Before I go any further I had better explain that as long as he lived in Othertime Scudamour found no difficulty in speaking and understanding a language which was certainly not English, but that he did not succeed in bringing a single word of this language back with him. Orfieu and MacPhee both regard this as confirming the theory that what occurred between him and his double was a real exchange of bodies. When Scudamour's consciousness entered the Othertime world it acquired no new knowledge in the strict sense of the word 'knowledge', but it found itself furnished with a pair of ears and a tongue and vocal chords that had been trained for years in receiving and making the sounds of the Othertime language, and a brain which was in the habit of associating those sounds with certain ideas. He thus simply found himself using a language which, in another sense, he did not 'know'. This view of the matter is borne out by the fact that if, in Othertime, he ever attempted to think what he was going to say, or even paused to choose a word, he at once became speechless. And if he failed to understand what an Othertimer said to him he could never lay his finger on any one word and ask what it meant. Their utterances had to be taken as a whole. When all went well, and when he was thinking hard of the subject-matter and not at all of the language, he could understand; but he could not take their talk to pieces linguistically or pick out nouns and verbs or anything of that sort.

'It's all right,' Scudamour repeated. 'I said I will not sting you.'

'I don't understand,' said the girl.

Scudamour's next remark failed. He had meant to say 'Thank God you don't,' but presumably there are no words for this in the language he was using. At this time he did not, of course, understand the linguistic situation which I have just described, and was astonished to find himself stammering. But his mind was racing on to other aspects of the situation.

'You know me, don't you?' he said.

'Of course I know you,' said the girl. 'You are the Lord of the Dark Tower and the Unicorn of the Eastern Plain.'

'But you know I have not always been this. You know who I am really. Camilla, don't you know *me*? You are Camilla still, aren't you, whatever they have done to us both?'

'I am Camilla,' said the girl.

Here I must interrupt again. It is not in the least likely that Scudamour really uttered the word 'Camilla' or that the girl uttered it in replying to him. Doubtless, he used whatever sound was associated with that woman in Othertime and got the same sound back from her. It would, of course, appear to him as the familiar name when he remembered the conversation after he got back to us, having recovered

65

his English-trained ears, brain, and tongue. But all this he did not understand at the time. Her reply confirmed him in his belief that the woman before him was the real Camilla Bembridge, caught like himself into the Othertime world.

'And who am I?' he asked.

'Why are you trying to entrap me?' said the girl. 'You know it is unlawful to speak to any unicorn as he was before – when he was only a common man.'

'I know nothing about their laws, Camilla. How can their laws change what is between you and me?'

She said nothing.

Scudamour came a step nearer. He was greatly bewildered and Camilla's replies seemed to be taking away the one thing that had been left him, for his sanity, in the wreck of his known world.

'Camilla,' he said, 'don't look at me like that! I have no idea what has happened to us both; but it can't mean that you no longer love me.'

The girl looked at him in amazement.

'You are mocking me,' she said. 'How can you love me now that you are what you are?'

'I don't want to be – this,' said Scudamour. 'I only want us both to get back, to be as we were. And if I stayed like this for a hundred years it would make no difference to my love for you – though I haven't much right to expect you to love me while I am . . . a unicorn. But can you not endure it for a time, till we get back? There must be a way back. We must be able to get across somehow.'

'Do you mean into the forest?' said the girl. 'You mean you would run away? Oh, but it is impossible. And the White Riders would kill us. But you are trying to entrap me. Leave me alone. I never said I would go. I never spoke your old name. I never said I still loved you. Why should you want me to be thrown into the fire?'

'I cannot understand a thing you are saying,' answered Scudamour. 'You seem to think I am your enemy. And you seem to know so much more than I do. Have you been here longer than I?'

'I have been here all my life.'

Scudamour groaned and put his hand to his head. A
second later he drew it away with a scream of agony. If
any doubt had lingered in his mind as to whether he bore
a sting on his forehead, here was proof positive. Only a
tiny drop of blood appeared on his hand, but he was dizzy
with the pain and he felt the poison tingling under his skin.
The terrible expectation that he would become a Jerky
arose in his mind; but apparently the body of a Stingingman is immune from the full effects of its own virus. His
hand was sore and swollen for several days but he was
otherwise unharmed. In the meantime the accident had
one result which he counted cheap at the price of the pain.
The tension in his head was relaxed, the throbbing grew
less, and the desire to sting disappeared. He felt once more
master of himself.

'Camilla, dear,' he said, 'something horrible has happened
to us both. I'll tell you what it seems like to me, and then
you must tell me what it has been like to you. But I am
afraid they have done something to your memory which
they haven't done to mine. Don't you remember any other
world – any other country – than this? Because I do. It
seems to me that until today you and I lived in a quite
different place where we wore different clothes and lived
in houses not at all like this. And we were lovers there
and were happy together. We had plenty of friends and
everyone was kind to us and wished us well. There were
no Stingingmen there and no Jerkies, and I had not got this
horrible thing in my head. Do you not remember all this?'

Camilla shook her head sadly.

'What do you remember?' he asked.

'I remember being here always,' she said. 'I remember
being a child, and I remember the day we first met, by
the broken bridge out there where the forest begins, and you
were only a boy and I was a little girl. And I remember
when Mother died and what you said to me the day after.
And then how happy we were, and all we thought we were
going to do, until the day when you changed.'

'But you remember me in all this, the real ME. You know who I am?'

The girl rose at this and looked him straight in the face. 'Yes,' she said. 'You are Michael.'

Once again, I do not suppose that the syllables she pronounced were really those I have written; but it seemed to Scudamour that he heard his own name. And it seemed to him that she spoke with the steadiness of a martyr, that she was putting her life in his hands. He partly understood then, and understood fully before he left that world, that if he had been the real Stingingman her mention of his name would have meant death to her. I gather that it was these words and her look while she spoke them that first raised in him any serious suspicion that she was not the real Camilla. He himself, as a loyal lover, could not explain why. The nearest he ever got to it was to say that the real Camilla was 'so sensible'. The rest of us, who had opportunities during his absence of getting to know the real Camilla pretty well, would put it more bluntly. She was not the sort of young woman who was likely to risk her life, or even her comfort, for the sake of truth in love or in anything else.

'You are right,' he said. 'You are Camilla and I am Michael, for ever and ever, whatever they do to us and however they confuse our minds. Hold fast to that. Can you believe what I have been telling you – that we don't belong here, we come from a better world and have got to go back there if we can?'

'It is very hard,' said the girl. 'But I will believe it if you tell me.'

'Good,' said Scudamour. 'Now tell me what you know about this world. You didn't seem to know why you had been brought here.'

'What do you mean? Of course I knew. I was coming here to drink of the fuller life, to be made a servant of the Big Brain. I was coming because my name had been called, and now that I had lost you I was glad enough.'

Scudamour hesitated. 'But, Camilla,' he said, 'when I told you I wasn't going to . . . to sting you – you didn't seem to understand.'

She started at his words and then stared at him with a face full of troubled wonder. You could see that the conceptions of a whole lifetime had been overturned. At last she spoke, almost in a whisper.

'So that is how it is really done!' she said.

'Do you mean to say they don't know?' he asked.

'None of us knew. No one sees a Stingingman when once he has been given his robe, or at least none of us common people. We do not know even where he is, though many stories are told. I did not know when I came into this room that I should find you here. We are told to come in never looking behind us and to make our prayer to . . . Him.' Here Camilla pointed over Scudamour's shoulder, and looking back he found himself face to face with the many-bodied idol which he had almost forgotten. Glancing at Camilla, he saw that she was bowing to it and moving her lips.

'Camilla, don't, don't,' said Scudamour hastily, moved by an impulse which he supposed to be irrational. She stopped and looked at him. Then gradually a blush came over her face and she dropped her eyes. Neither of them, perhaps, understood why.

'Go on,' said Scudamour presently.

'We are told,' said Camilla, 'to pray to his image, and then he himself will come from behind us and lay his hundred hands upon our heads and breathe into us the greater life so that we shall live no longer with our own life but with his. No one has ever dreamed it was the Unicorn-man. We were told you bore stings not for us but for our enemies.'

'But do those who have been through it never tell?'

'How could they tell?'

'Why not?'

'But they don't speak.'

'You mean they are dumb?' said Scudamour.

'They are – I don't know how it is with them,' said the girl. 'They go about their business needing no words because they live with a single life higher than their own. They are above speech.'

'Poor creatures,' said Scudamour half to himself.

'Do you mean they are not happy?' said the girl. 'Is that a lie too?'

'Happy?' said Scudamour. 'I don't know. Not with any kind of happiness that concerns you and me.'

'We are told that one moment of their life is such bliss that it surpasses all the best and sweetest that we others could experience in a thousand years.'

'You don't believe that?'

'I don't want it.'

She looked at him with eyes full of love. He thought to himself that Camilla had not loved him so well in the old world. He did not dare to draw near and kiss her, his sting forbade him. No doubt he could turn his head aside – the thing could be managed, but he felt a certain horror at the idea of bringing his face, as it now was, close to hers.

There was silence between them for a minute or so. He saw that he must learn much more of this strange country and that they must make plans; but the very depth of this ignorance and the number of questions he wanted to ask kept him from beginning. As he stood thus he gradually became aware that there was a great deal of noise going on outside the Dark Tower and that it was rapidly increasing. Ever since he had entered Othertime there had, indeed, been a good deal of distant noise – noises of hammering and workmen's calls, as he now realized, though he had not hitherto attended to them. But these had disappeared. What he now heard was more like confusion and riot. There were shouts and cheers mixed with sudden silences and then the tread of many feet moving in haste.

'Do you know what is happening?' he said, at the same time glancing quickly round the room and noticing that the windows – unglazed, oblong windows – were high above his head and gave him no chance of seeing out.

Before Camilla could reply the door was suddenly flung open – not one of the doors on the dais, but the door at the far end where the stone seats were. A man dashed into the room, and sinking on one knee with such haste that he seemed to have fallen, cried out, 'The White Riders, Lord! The White Riders are upon us!'

6

Scudamour had no time to consider his reply, and that was what saved him. Almost without the co-operation of his will he found himself answering in the firm, cold voice of one accustomed to command, 'Well. Do you not know your duties?'

His body was repeating some lesson that its nerves and muscles had learned before he had entered it; and it was a complete success. The newcomer flinched a little like a scolded dog and said in a humbler voice, 'Yes, Lord. There are no new orders?'

'There are no new orders,' answered Scudamour with perfect outward composure, and the man, bowing low, instantly disappeared. For the first time since he had passed through the chronoscope Scudamour felt inclined to laugh; he was beginning to enjoy the gigantic game of bluff which would apparently be forced on him. At the same time he was greatly puzzled by the appearance of this man, who did not seem to fall into any of the categories of the Othertime society which he already knew. Scudamour could only describe him as a stingless Stingingman. He had all the appearances of the stinging caste except the sting – black robes, black hair, and pallid face.

He would have asked Camilla who and what the man was, but the sounds from without were such as now claimed all his attention. He heard more cheering, angry voices, cries of pain, tinkling of steel on steel, and, above all, the thunder of hoofs. 'I must see this,' he said. 'Perhaps if I stood on the chair – ', but the chair was either fixed to the floor or else too heavy to move and he could not drag it under the windows. He went to the far end of the room and stood on the stone seat; then back to the dais and stood on it. He stood on tiptoes and craned his neck, but could see nothing but the sky. The noise was increasing. Clearly something like a full battle was in progress. There were great thudding shocks now as if the enemy were battering the door of the Dark Tower itself.

'Who are these White Riders?' he said.

'Oh, Michael,' said Camilla with a gesture of despair, 'have you forgotten even that? They are the savages, the man-eaters, who have destroyed nearly all the world.'

'Nearly all the world?'

'Of course. And now they have come here too – half the island is in their hands. But you must know that. That is why more and more of us must give ourselves to the Big Brain, and why we must work longer and live harder – we are only a remnant. Our backs are to a wall. When they have killed us they will have destroyed the whole world of man.'

'I see,' said Scudamour. 'I see. I knew nothing about this.' It was indeed a wholly new light to him. In studying Othertime through the chronoscope he had been absorbed in the sheer evil, as it seemed to him, of what he saw; it had not occurred to him to inquire into its origins – perhaps, its excuses.

'But, Camilla,' he said, 'if they are only savages why have we not defeated them?'

'I don't know,' she said. 'They are so many, and so big. They are harder to kill than we are. And they grow so fast. We have few children, they have many. I do not understand much about it.'

'The noise seems to be dying down. Do you think our men are all killed?' He was horrified to find that he had called the Othertimers 'our men'.

'There would be more noise if the Riders had got into the Tower,' said Camilla.

'That's true,' said Scudamour. 'Perhaps they are beaten.'

'Perhaps they were not very many. This is the first time

72

they have come here. Next time there will be more of them.'

'Listen!' said Scudamour suddenly. There seemed to be almost complete silence in the outer world now, and in the silence a single voice, crying out very loud and somewhat monotonously as if a proclamation were being made. He could not catch what it was saying. Then came again the noise of trampling hoofs, this time gradually diminishing.

'They have gone,' said Camilla.

'It sounds like it,' said Scudamour, 'and that may be as bad for you and me, dear, as if they had won. That man will be back any minute. Now what am I to do about you? Will they let me keep you here now that I haven't stung you?'

'If you tell them I am not fit to be made a servant of the Big Brain they will put me into the fire.'

The words recalled Scudamour sharply to reality. He would not call such creatures 'our men' a second time.

'But what if I say you are to be kept here – just as you are?'

She looked at him wonderingly.

[Here folio 49 of the manuscript is missing.]

be a sad people.'

'I dare say, I dare say. And perhaps a jealous, envious, malicious people too.'

'You are teaching me all the time to say things that we do not dare to think.'

'Listen!' said Scudamour. The door opened again and the same black-robed attendant appeared.

'Hail, Lord,' he began, sinking on his knee. 'As no one doubted, you have overcome the barbarians and spread the terror of your name among them.'

'Tell your story,' said Scudamour.

'They came out of the wood from the north,' said the man, 'galloping so fast that your scouts were hardly here before them, and they were on us before the troops could

73

well be ordered. They came straight to the north door and some of them dismounted; they had a felled tree for a battering-ram. They seemed to take no notice of the workmen who caught up what they could for weapons and came at them. The Riders were more ready to threaten them than to fight, and when the workmen would not be kept back by threats they struck feebly and like fools – even using the butts of their lances. They killed very few. When the troops came, it was another matter. The Riders charged them with lances and drove them back twice. Then they seemed to lose heart and would not charge a third time. They left off battering the door and drew together and then their leader shouted out a message. Then they fled.'

Scudamour gathered from the appearance of the messenger that he had not been in the engagement himself. He also began to think that the Othertimers had odd ideas of what constituted a victory.

'What was the message?' he asked.

The man appeared embarrassed. 'It is not fit . . .' he began. 'It was full of vile blasphemies.'

'What was the message?' Scudamour repeated in the same tone.

'The Lord of the Dark Tower would doubtless like to hear it in secret,' said the man, who had already glanced several times at Camilla. Then, as if taking his courage in both hands, he added, 'And this woman, Lord? She has not yet drunk of the fuller life? Doubtless the Lord was interrupted by the coming of the Riders.'

'She is not going to taste of that life at present,' said Scudamour boldly.

'She goes to the fire, then?' said the man carelessly.

'No,' replied Scudamour, carefully keeping all emotion out of his voice. 'I have other work for her to do. She must be lodged here in my apartments, and, listen, she is to be treated no worse than myself.'

He regretted the last words as soon as he said them – it would have been wiser, he thought, to show no particular solicitude. He could not read the man's face. He supposed

74

it would be thought he intended Camilla for his mistress, and had little fear lest her wishes in the matter might count for anything in the Othertime social system; but he did not know whether such things were in the character of a Stingingman.

'To hear is to obey,' said the attendant, and rising, opened the door, and motioned to Camilla to follow him. It was not what either of them wished and there was no opportunity to exchange words. At all costs, he must arouse no unnecessary suspicion. Camilla hesitated and went.

Left alone, Scudamour suffered a sudden reaction from the strain of the last hour. He found that his legs were trembling and sank into his chair. He tried to think out his next move. It would have been easier if his head had not ached so.

The respite lasted only a few minutes and then the attendant returned. He knelt as before but there was a subtle change in his voice as he began.

'It went roughly, as I have already told you. They tried to spare the workmen as they always do, and the workmen had no taste for coming within the reach of their lances. When the Jerkies came, it was as always. They do not seem to know how to get out of the way of the horses. Do what we will, we cannot make them move like real men and change their direction. They go on as they are set all right.'

'And what of the message?'

'Oh it was the same they have given elsewhere, that whoever comes to them – the Lord of the Tower will forgive me – whoever comes to them with a sting in his hand, cut from a Unicorn's head, shall have a good welcome, he and all his party, and be a great man among them. I am afraid many of the people heard it.'

'It is no matter,' said Scudamour. That cryptic remark came readily off his tongue and served well enough, but he found himself very much at a loss for something more to say when the attendant began again.

'And the woman, Lord?' he said tentatively.

'Well,' said Scudamour, 'what of the woman?'

'Surely she was not wrongly chosen for stinging. All care was taken. They are very like.'

The last words electrified Scudamour. They bore to him an obvious sense – that the Othertime woman was like Camilla Bembridge in his own time, or, as he preferred to think, that there had once been two such doubles, though now, somehow or other, Camilla was imprisoned with him in the wrong world. It had not occurred to him that the Othertimer would know this. The intense complexity of the problem rushed suddenly upon his mind and made him speechless. But he must not stop to think now – at all costs he must avoid a silence. At last he said sternly, 'There are other things to be done before that.'

The man looked hard at him. 'The Lord will remember that such things do not end well for the Unicorn who tries them.' Then, after a short pause, he added, 'But the Lord need not fear *me*. I will keep his secret. I am his son and his daughter.'

In our world the words would hardly have been uttered without some sort of confidential leer, but even the mask-like gravity of the speaker's face could not conceal his meaning. It is, I think, a rather curious fact that Scudamour felt a quite old-fashioned desire to hit the man hard in the face – an old-fashioned, if you will a Victorian, indignation as at an insult to Camilla. For the real Camilla Bembridge was what is called 'modern'. She was so free to talk about the things her grandmother could not mention that Ransom once said he wondered if she were free to talk about any-thing else. There would have been no difficulty about sug-gesting to her that she might become your mistress; I do not think you would have succeeded unless you offered very good security, but there would have been no tears or blushes or indignation. And Scudamour, one gathers, had taken his tone from her. But here he felt different. Perhaps he had never been so very 'modern' in his heart. At all events he now felt a strong desire to hit that man. The idea of sharing a secret, and such a secret, with him was infuriating. He relapsed into his haughtiest manner.

'You are a fool,' he said. 'How should you know what is in my mind? It is more a question how long I shall keep *your* secret, or whether I am ready to forget that you have spoken thus.' At this moment an inspiration came to Scudamour. It was very risky and if he had had time to weigh the risks he might not have acted on it. He turned to the broken chronoscope. 'Does this mean nothing to you?' he said. 'Do you think nothing out of the ordinary is now to be planned and done?'

The man opened his eyes wider – perhaps he was genuinely impressed. 'I am your son and your daughter,' he said. 'Have *they* broken it?'

Scudamour made a motion of his head which, he hoped, might at need be interpreted as a sign of assent or as a mere pensive refusal to answer.

'Have I the Lord's leave to speak?' said the man.

'Speak,' said Scudamour.

'Does the Lord think of using the woman's brain? Would it not be wasteful? Would not any common brain do as well?'

Scudamour started. He knew that Orfieu had had great trouble in finding a preparation equivalent to the Z substance in the 'human brain – a necessary element in his chronoscope. Obviously the Othertimers had a simpler method.

'You do not understand in the least what is to be done,' he said coldly. All through the conversation he had been reminding himself that it was foolish to begin by insulting and antagonizing the first Othertime man he had met, but he was continually being forced to do so. His only asset in this new world was his official superiority as a Stingingman and the only means of disguising his ignorance was to play that superiority for all it was worth. But he felt that he was now very nearly at the end of his tether.

'Bring me some food,' he said.

'Here, Lord?' said the attendant, apparently in some surprise.

Scudamour hesitated. His chief purpose in asking for food had been to get a few moments alone, but it now occurred to him that he had better begin as soon as possible to explore – to find out what rooms and passages surrounded him.

'Set me food in the usual place,' he said.

The attendant rose and opened the door, standing aside for Scudamour to pass. Much as he hated the carved room, he did not cross the threshold without a tremor, for he had no idea what he might encounter. He found himself in a much larger room – an oblong hall of patterned stone with many doors. At one end of it some dozen or fifteen of the stingless Stingingmen were seated close together on the floor. They rose and bowed low, or even prostrated themselves, as he appeared, but he had time to notice that they had all been whispering with their heads close together and busily examining a miscellaneous litter of objects which strewed the floor about them as toys strew the floor about a child. Indeed they were such things as a child might well have used for playing shop. There were little boxes and jars and bowls, bottles, tubes, packets, and tiny spoons.

Scudamour learned much later what all this meant, but it may as well be mentioned here. The truth is that the stingless relatives of the Stingingmen – the Drones, as we may call them – have only one interest in life. They are all hoping to grow stings. They spend nearly all their spare time in the laboratory, concocting every kind of nostrum which they think may produce the coveted deformity. Sometimes it is drugs to drink, sometimes powders and plasters for the forehead, sometimes incisions and cauterizations. One depends on diet, another on some kind of exercises. Scudamour says they reminded him of nothing so much as of the inveterate gamblers whom one finds living in the neighbourhood of any big continental casino – every one with an infallible private recipe for making his fortune. And like the gamblers they seemed to have a hope which no experience could overthrow. Very few of them, perhaps none, as far as he could learn, had ever succeeded. Year after year they watched young men on whom the caprice of nature had lavished the sting succeeding to the seats of power while they themselves grew old amid their experiments. Often if Scudamour came suddenly into the ante-room he heard fragments of their whispered conversation – 'When my sting has grown,' 'Now that I have found the real treatment,' 'Of course it is almost certain that I shall not be with you next year.'

The attendant led him through this hall and into another, smaller, room, where he noted with disappointment the same high windows. The food was brought him here. To his relief, the attendant showed no tendency to remain and wait on him.

Presumably the body which Scudamour now animated had not fed for some time, and he found himself turning to his meal with alacrity. He was thirsty as well as hungry and raised eagerly to his lips a silver cup which appeared to be full of water. A moment later he set it down in astonishment. There may have been some water in it, but most of the mixture was some kind of spirit, a raw, fiery liquid that left the mouth parched. He was surprised that he did not dislike it more. He then found that he had taken up a fruit from the plate before him and was beginning to eat it with the ease of long habit. It was rather like a persimmon and he could not at first understand the relish with which he ate it, for he had always disliked persimmons. From this he proceeded to a dry, grey concoction in a wooden bowl. It consisted of small grey particles, many of them gritty in texture. The whole meal, indeed, was of a dry, choleric, and adust nature; and all the time he enjoyed what he ate with a curious feeling that it was unnatural to enjoy it. Only when his hunger was three parts satisfied did he realize the explanation. He was experiencing the pleasures of an alien body; the palate and stomach which liked these foods and were habituated to them, did not belong to him. And with the discovery there came a sense of horror. Perhaps this was the very diet on which the venom of a Stingingman was maintained. Perhaps

. . . he was not sure that there might not have been insects, or worse, in that grey mixture. He pushed his chair back from the table and rose. He was trying to remember something – some warning in a fairy tale heard long before he went to school. He could not quite recapture it, but it was borne in upon him that he had better eat as little of such food as he could. He wondered how much suspicion it would arouse if he asked for something else. In the meantime he must find out where they had put Camilla.

He came out into the oblong hall, and the same attendant rose from where he had been sitting among the other Drones and came to him. In answer to his questions the man explained, as far as he could make out, that he had put Camilla in Scudamour's own bedroom. He spoke almost in a whisper and the desire to put himself on a confidential footing with his master was clearer than before. His manner was a shade less deferential and more insinuating. Scudamour again took a high line. He made the man lead him to Camilla – and thus incidentally discovered his own room – and then find other lodging for her. They were not able to speak to one another alone or even to exchange incautious glances, but at least each now knew where the other was housed. Scudamour was surprised at the number of sleeping chambers and wondered who the usual guests of a Stingingman might be. After he had given fresh orders that Camilla should be well cared for and not molested he made a tour of all the rooms. He was followed everywhere by his attendant and by the eyes of all the Drones. This was not pleasant and he felt that what he was doing might raise their wonder. But it had to be risked, since the first condition of any possible plan was a knowledge of his surroundings. What he mainly wanted to find was the way out of his own apartments – at any moment it might become desirable to leave the Dark Tower in haste. In this he was not successful : room opened into room interminably and long before he had exhausted the possibilities he decided that, on this occasion at any rate, he dared not continue the search any further. In the meantime, however, he had found a library – a room as large as the anteroom and lined with books to the ceiling. He did not suppose at this stage that he would be able to read them, but he welcomed the library as a pretext for shaking off the Drone, and he wanted to rest.

7

'I wish Ransom were here,' said Scudamour to himself. Ransom is a philologist. Scudamour knows little about languages and scrips, and a glance at the characters on the backs of the books convinced him that he would never be able to decipher them. He had not expected that he would, and sat down at once to consider his situation. Two ideas were, at this stage, contending in his mind. The first was the possibility of repairing the chronoscope and returning by the way he had come. This was beset with difficulties. He knew it would take Orfieu, on *our* side, a long time to make a new chronoscope and he rightly assumed that two instruments, one in each time, were necessary. Nor was he at all clear how he could get Camilla through with him. His other idea was much nearer to despair – a vague hope that if return were impossible, escape, and escape with Camilla, from the Dark Tower into the territories of the White Riders might be managed. He was fairly certain that these barbarians were more human than the Stinging people, and that some life not utterly detestable might be lived among them. But then he remembered their proclamation and thought that what he bore in his forehead would exclude him, of all people, from any alliance with them. And with that reflection a rebellious horror at the monstrosity he had now become surged over him anew, and he rose and paced the silent room in his anguish.

Then came a surprise. He had taken perhaps six or seven turns in this fashion when, hardly noticing that he had done so, he paused at one end of his walk, took a volume from the shelves, and to his astonishment found that he had read a line or two with ease. Of course he ought to have anticipated this. The body which he was using had already so paced in that library, so paused, and so taken down a book; and Scudamour's mind, using the Stingingman's eyes, could read his books for the very same reasons which enabled him to use the Othertime language. It was only his own doubts and his own conscious efforts which had prevented him from understanding their titles when he first entered the library.

The lines he had read were as follows: 'It must be remembered that even the instructed had, at this period, no conception of the real nature of time. The world, for them, had a unilinear history from which there was no escape, as it has for the common people to the present day. It was therefore very natural that — '

The passage went on to some historical matter that did not interest him. Hastily he turned over several pages, but the book seemed to be all historical and he saw no more references to the subject of time. He was beginning to wonder whether he should sit down and read the book from the beginning when he discovered that it had an index. Fortunately he was now too excited to stop and ask himself whether he knew the Othertime alphabet. He found the word 'time' easily enough, but the only passage mentioned under it turned out to be the one he had already read. For a moment his researches were at a standstill. Then he discovered that the book he held in his hands was one of a series, a history in many volumes. He put it back and tried the volume on his right, but a few minutes of comparison convinced him that it dealt, not with a later, but with an earlier period. Perhaps the Othertimers put books on a shelf in what we regard as the wrong order. He tried a volume to the left and could not at first discover whether his surmise was correct. The business was going to take him longer than he thought, and he had to master the concluding pages of the original volume fairly thoroughly. They dealt with a history absolutely unknown to him. Some people called the Darkeners were being suppressed 'with great but necessary severities', though whether they were a sect, a nation, or a powerful family he could not discover. He learned enough, however, to enable him to decide that the volume to the left was the sequel. He went to its index and found about twenty references to 'time,' but all of the same cryptic character. The reader was constantly reminded that 'complete ignorance on this fundamental subject still prevailed', that 'the monistic view of time which immediate experience seems to suggest had not yet been called in question', or that 'the detestable superstitions of the Dark Age still found a foothold in the pessimistic view of time then current', and this sent him post-haste to the next volume. Feeling sure that he was now approaching the heart of the mystery, he carried it to a table in the centre of the room and sat down to read in earnest.

The index to this volume bristled with entries under the heading that interested him. He tried the first and learned that 'the new conception of time was destined to remain for centuries of purely theoretical interest, but this should not lead us to underrate its effects'. He turned on: 'As has already been pointed out, the revolution in our knowledge of time had as yet given us no power to control it, but it had profoundly modified the human mind.' There were dozens of similar statements and Scudamour, more accustomed to laboratories than to libraries, began to feel impatient. In despair he turned back to the first page of the book and after reading a few lines flung it from him in anger; for he had seen that it began with the statement that 'this was not the place' for an account of those discoveries with whose historical results the following pages were mainly concerned.

'They expect you to know,' said Scudamour drily. Then he picked up the volume, replaced it, and began studying other titles. Many of them were unintelligible to him. He realized that any of them, or none of them, might contain what he wanted to know, and that he would not have time – at least he hoped he would not have time – to read the whole library.

A book with a title like *The Nature of Things* looked

promising, and the contents held his attention for some time, not because they proved helpful but because they amazed him. Whatever these people knew about time, they knew very little about space. He read that the earth was the shape of a saucer, and that you could not reach the edge of the saucer because you slipped down the incline 'as the experience of sailors shows,' that the sun was twenty miles high, and that stars were 'inflammations of the air.' Somehow this ignorance comforted him. The next book – *Time Angles* – had the opposite effect. It began: 'An uncontrolled time proceeding in the backward-forward direction is subject, as is known, to fluctuations during which small extensions of it (say .05 of a second) will make a measurable angle with the backward-forward direction. If, now, we suppose this increased to a right angle, this time will proceed from eckward to andward' – so the words appeared to Scudamour's memory when he told us the story – 'and will cut an ideally normal time at right angles. At the B moment of intersection the whole series of events in each of these times will then be contemporary to those living in the other.'

Was this nonsense? The childishness of Othertime geography suggested that it might be little better, but then a disquieting thought struck him. How if this race had specialized in the knowledge of time, and ours in the knowledge of space? Might not our conceptions of time, in that event, be as erroneous as the Othertimers' saucer earth and airy stars? Scudamour's own astronomical conceptions would appear as absurd in Othertime as this strange doctrine of temporal angles and fluctuations appeared to him; it would not therefore be untrue. He read on.

'Let the moment of intersection be X. X will then be a historical moment common to both the times; in other words the total state of the universe in time A at moment X will be identical with the total state of the universe in time B at moment X. Now like states or events have like results. Therefore the whole future of time A (that is, its whole content in the forward direction) will duplicate the whole future of time B (that is its whole content in the andward direction).'

Scudamour fancied that he already knew something about duplications; eagerly he turned the page. 'Here,' said the book, 'we are speaking of uncontrolled times; the reader will naturally seek elsewhere for an account of those controlled times which are, of course, of more obvious practical importance.' Scudamour was only too ready to seek elsewhere. If the library were systematically arranged, the book he wanted must be somewhere near. He took down several volumes. All were concerned with the same subject and in all of them a meaning which he could not seize was implicit. He had almost turned away from this section of the library in despair when at last he took down a book apparently somewhat older than its fellows which stood in the highest shelf and which he had more than once already passed over as unpromising. It had some such title as *First Principles*.

'It was anciently believed,' he read, 'that space had three dimensions and time but one, and our fathers commonly pictured time as a stream or a thin cord, the present being a moving point on that cord or a floating leaf on that stream. The direction backward from the present was called the past, as it still is, and the direction forward the future. What is a little more remarkable is that only one such stream or cord was believed to exist, and that the universe was thought to contain no other events or states than those which occupied, at some point or other, the stream or cord along which our own present is travelling. There were not lacking, indeed, philosophers who pointed out that this was merely a fact of experience and that we could give no reason why time had only one dimension and why there was only a single time; indeed more than one of the early chronologists hazarded the idea that time might itself be a dimension of space – an idea which will seem almost fantastically perverse to us, but which, in their state of knowledge, deserved the praise of ingenuity. In general, however, such interest as the ancients took in time was diverted from fruitful inquiries by their vain efforts to discover means of what they called "time-travel", by which they meant nothing more than reversal or acceleration of the mind's movement along our own unilinear time.

'This is not the place' (here Scudamour groaned again) 'to describe the experiments which, in the thirtieth year of the tenth era, convinced chronologists that the time in which we live has lateral fluctuations; in other words that the cord or stream is not to be represented by a straight but by a wavy line. It is difficult for us to realize how revolutionary this discovery at first appeared. So deeply rooted were the old conceptions that we read of thinkers who could not conceive such fluctuation. They inquired in *what,* or into *what,* the time cord deviated when it deviated from the straight; and their reluctance to allow the obvious answer (that it deviated in, or into time, in an eckwards or andwards direction) gave a new lease of life to the perverse doctrine we have already noted, which was now called the doctrine of Space Time.

'Not until the year 47 do we find any clear understanding of the truth, but by 51 – '

What followed was a proper name which Scudamour has been unable to tell us, though he recognized it as a proper name while he read. It was one doubtless as familiar to Othertime ears as those of Copernicus and Darwin are to ours; but 'X' is the best I can do for it here.

' – by 51 X had produced a map of time which was essentially correct as far as it went. His time is two-dimensional – a plane which he represented on the map as a square but which he then believed to be of infinite extension. The backwards-forwards direction was from left to right, the eckwards-andwards from top to bottom. Across this our time is shown as a wavy line running predominantly from left to right. Other times, which to him were merely theoretical, are represented by dotted lines running in the same direction above and below – that is to the eckwards and andwards of our time. This diagram was at first the cause of dangerous misunderstandings, which X himself did his best to combat when he published his great *Timebook* in 57. In it he pointed out that though all the times were diagrammatically represented as starting from the left-hand or backward side of the square, it must not therefore be assumed that they had a beginning in something timeless. To do so would, in fact, be to forget that the left-hand side of the square must itself represent a time-line. Let the square which represents the plane of two-dimensional time be ABCD, and let XY and OP be two time-lines traversing it in the eckward-andward direction. It is clear that if AB and DC represent any reality – that is, if the square is not infinite as he had at first supposed – they also will be time-

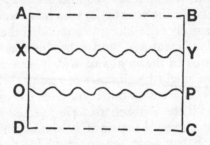

lines. But it is no less clear that the same is true of AD and BC. There will be times proceeding either from eckwards to andwards or from andwards to eckwards. In that case X and O, which from our point of view are the beginnings of time itself, are in fact simply moments, successive to one another in the AD time. And if the directions of all the four times run the right way – i.e. from A to B, B to C, C to D, D to A – then a consciousness which succeeded in passing, say at Y, from the XY time to the BC, and at C from the BC time to the CD, and so on, would attain to endless time, and the Time Square, though finite, would be endless or perpetual ...'

'I don't believe a word of it!' ejaculated Scudamour suddenly, looking up from the book, and then checking himself in some surprise. He had not been prepared for the distaste which had been aroused in him by the kind of immortality which the Othertimers apparently welcomed with enthusiasm. 'I'd sooner be snuffed out,' he found himself thinking. 'I'd sooner go to a heaven of harps and angels like what they used to tell me about when I was a boy.' (No one had, in fact, told him any such thing, but he was under a not uncommon delusion on this subject.) 'I'd sooner have anything than go round and round that way like a rat in a bucket of water.' 'But it might be true all the same,' whispered his scientific consciousness. He turned once more to the book and read on. After a few pages he found the following.

'It was left to X's successors to find the practical bearing of his discovery. In the year 6o Z, who had come to chronology from the study of folklore, propounded the theory that certain fabulous creatures, and other images which constantly appeared in the myths of widely separated peoples and in dreams, might be glimpses of realities which exist in a time closely adjacent to our own. This led to his famous experiment with the Smokehorse. He selected this familiar horror of the nursery because it is almost unique among such images in having arisen in historical times – no evidence having been found of its existence before the last century. By the psychological technique which has since become famous he found that he could produce the Smokehorse, first as a dream, and later as a waking hallucination, in his own consciousness and that of the children on whom he experimented. But he also found that it had altered in various ways from the Smokehorse of tradition, and even from that of his own earliest memories. The old Smokehorse – still favoured in popular art – consists essentially of a small cylindrical body supported on four wheels, and the conspicuous tall spout which emits the smoke. But the Smokehorses seen by Z had very much larger bodies, usually of green, and eight or ten wheels, while the spout had been reduced to a tiny protuberance on the front of the cylindrical body. By 66 he had discovered a feature of which tradition and uncontrolled dreams had given no hint, and which therefore put it beyond doubt that he was dealing with some objective reality. He was able to observe that the Smokehorses in drawing their gigantic loads of wheeled vehicles proceeded not along the earth, as had been supposed, but along parallel rods of smooth metal, and that this was the real explanation of their prodigious speed.'

Scudamour, in spite of himself, was now reading too rapidly to take in the full sense of what he read. The next passage that he can remember was something like this.

'By 69 Z had succeeded in making something like a map of certain portions of our native land as they are in Othertime. The steel roads on which the Smokehorses travel, and which could be comparatively easily traced, gave him his first bearings. He detected the huge Othertime city which occupies what, in our time, are the marshes at the beginning of the Eastwater estuary and traced a complete Smokehorse road from this to our City of the Eastern Plain. More than this he was unable to do because of the conditions under which he worked. He had rightly chosen children as his chief instruments for the inspection of Othertime, because in them the mind is less preoccupied by the ideas and images of our own existence. The experiences of these children had very disagreeable effects, leading to extreme terror and finally to insanity, and most of those whom he used had to be destroyed before they reached maturity. The morals of the period were low – the White Riders had not yet reached even the continental coast – and the government was weak and short-sighted : Z was forbidden to use any children of the more intelligent stocks, foolish restrictions were placed on his disciplinary control of those allotted to him, and in the year 70 this great pioneer fell a victim to assassination.'

'Thank –' said Scudamour and then stopped short. The word he had intended was not to be found. He read on.

'The honours of the next stage in this great discovery are divided between K and Q. K, who worked in the Southwestern region, concentrated his attention entirely on stationary Smokehorses, of which large collections could be experienced in his area. At first he used adult criminals rather than children, but already the possibility of a different method had occurred to him. He decided to construct in our own time the nearest replica he could of an Othertime Smokehorse. He failed repeatedly because the Othertimers invariably moved their Smokehorse before his model was completed. By this time, however, K had been able to observe the Othertime building in which the stationary Smokehorses were usually kept. With indefatigable patience he set himself to duplicate it in our own time – of course in the exact *space* occupied by the Othertime building. The results surpassed all expectation. Smokehorses and even Othertime human beings now became faintly, but continuously, visible even to untrained observers. The whole theory of time attraction was thus brought into being, and formulated in K's law that "Any two time-lines approximate in the exact degree to which their material contents are alike." It had now become possible, as it were, to bring ourselves at will within sight of an alien time; it still remained to find whether we could produce any effect on it – whether we were within striking distance. K solved the problem by his celebrated "Exchange". He succeeded in observing an Othertime girl, aged about ten, and living with her parents, under the conditions of extraordinary indulgence which, in Othertime, both the state and the family seem to allow. He then took one of our own children, of the same age and sex, and, as nearly as possible, of the same physical type, and caused it to become conscious of its Othertime counterpart – specially at times when the experiences of the latter would be likely to attract it. At the same time, he treated it with the greatest severity. Having thus produced in its mind a strong wish to change places with the Othertimer, he juxtaposed them, while the latter was asleep, and simply ordered the this-time child to escape him if it could. The experiment succeeded. The child fell asleep and woke with, apparently, no knowledge of its surroundings, and, at first, no fear of K. It continued to ask for its mother, and to beg that it might be allowed to "go home".

Every kind of test was applied, and no doubt need be felt that a real exchange of personalities had taken place. The alien child thus taken from Othertime proved unamenable to our educational methods and was finally used for scientific purposes.'

Scudamour got up and took a turn or two up and down the room. He noticed that the daylight was beginning to fade, and he felt tired, but not at all hungry. His mind was curiously divided – on one side a raging torrent of curiosity, on the other a deep reluctance to read further. The curiosity won, and he sat down again.

'Meanwhile,' the book continued, 'Q had been experimenting with the possibilities of some inanimate instrument which might give us a view of Othertime without the need of the old precarious psychological exertions. In 74 he produced his

[The manuscript breaks off here at the foot of folio 64.]

A NOTE ON
THE DARK TOWER

by Walter Hooper

After an unavailing search for more pages, I showed this fragment to Major Lewis, Owen Barfield and Roger Lancelyn Green and was disappointed to learn that they had never seen or heard of it. When Roger Lancelyn Green and I were writing *C. S. Lewis: A Biography* (1974) no one else had seen it, or recognized our description of it in the biography, and I wrongly concluded that it had never been read to the Inklings – the group of friends who met in Lewis's Magdalen College rooms each Thursday evening during term. But, then, Lewis's friend Gervase Mathew read the manuscript and recognized it at once. He remembers hearing Lewis read the first four chapters at a meeting of the Inklings in 1939 or 1940, and he recalls that the Inklings' discussion of these chapters centred mainly on the subjects of time and memory, both of which held a strong fascination for Lewis at the time.

Lewis's friends, and almost everyone else in Oxford, would have understood his references, in the first chapter, to the 'English ladies at Trianon' who 'saw a whole scene from a part of the past long before their birth' and the book by 'Dunne'. But they are not well known today and some clarification is probably needed. The 'English ladies' were Miss Charlotte Anne Elizabeth Moberley (1846-1937), the Principal of St Hugh's College, Oxford, from 1886 to 1915, and Miss Eleanor Frances Jourdain (1863-1924), who was Principal of the same college from 1915 to 1924. These distinguished and learned ladies won considerable notoriety in Oxford by publishing in 1911, under the pseudonyms 'Elizabeth Morison' and 'Frances Lamont', a fascinating book called *An Adventure* – which 'adventure' consisted of their seeing, on their first visit to the Petit Trianon on

10 August 1901, the palace and gardens exactly as they believed they would have appeared to Marie Antoinette in 1792.

This extraordinary ghost-story is not, perhaps, unbelievable, and I understand that Lewis did believe it till, some time later, his friend Dr R. E. Havard mentioned having seen a retraction of it by one of the ladies involved. Lewis had not, till then, heard of any such disclaimer and Dr Havard says that he was 'disinclined to accept it'. Though Dr Havard is not the only person to believe there had been a retraction (Professor Tolkien was another), the people who know most about Miss Moberley and Miss Jourdain seem never to have heard of it. That being the case, and till there is strong evidence to the contrary, it is perhaps wise to conclude that the ladies stuck to their story for the rest of their lives. While it would appear that Lewis believed the ladies' testimony while he was writing *The Dark Tower,* he did not end as he began. Near the end of his life he thought Miss Jourdain's statements were unreliable.

The other book mentioned in the first chapter, and which struck fire from Lewis's imagination, is *An Experiment with Time* (1927) by John William Dunne, an aeronautical experimenter and the exponent of Serialism. In Part III of his book Dunne suggests that all dreams are composed of images of past experience and images of future experience blended together in approximately equal proportions. In order to corroborate this, he suggests – and this is the 'experiment' Orfieu refers to on page 22 – that one keep a notebook and pencil under one's pillow, and that '*immediately* on waking, before you even open your eyes, you set yourself to remember the rapidly vanishing dream', with the result that, if such a diary is kept over a sufficiently long period, the experimenter will discover such a blending of past and future events. It should be noted, however, that whereas Dunne is saying that a man can, under certain conditions, glance backwards and forwards within his own life, Orfieu is combining this with the belief that you may see into other people's lives – as the St Hugh's ladies claim to have done through the mind of the French queen.

Lewis himself had a great many dreams, and experienced frequent occurrences of *dé jà vu*. As, however, his dreams were often nightmares, which he seemed more anxious to forget than remember, I doubt if he attempted Dunne's 'experiment'. During the course of the Inklings meeting, and in a subsequent talk with Gervase Mathew in Addison's Walk (of Magdalen College), Lewis said he believed that *dé jà vu* consisted in 'seeing' what you – you only – had at some time merely dreamed.

On the second of these occasions Gervase Mathew suggested that memory, which at times seems to involve precognition, might be an inherited gift, a legacy from one's ancestors. How far Lewis went along with this it is difficult to say, but the idea appears to have lodged in his mind to come out later in *That Hideous Strength,* where Jane Studdock has inherited the Tudor gift of second sight, the ability to dream realities. Even the notion of an 'Othertime', which is neither our past, present nor future, was to find its way into his later books – most notably *The Chronicles of Narnia.* Closer to the time *The Dark Tower* was written, the ideas found expression in *That Hideous Strength* (ch. IX, part v), in which the following explanation is offered as to where Merlin was from the fifth century till he woke in the twentieth : 'Merlin had not died. His life had been hidden, sidetracked, moved out of one-dimensional time, for fifteen centuries . . . in that place where those things remain that are taken off time's main-road, behind the invisible hedges, into the unimaginable fields. Not all the times that are outside the present are therefore past or future.'

While *The Dark Tower* tells us a great deal about C. S. Lewis's reflections on time, I think it would be a mistake to suppose that fact and fiction, so finely blended in his story, were not clearly distinguished in his mind. Indomitable Christian supernaturalist though he was, the truth is that, while he saw the interesting possibilities psychic phenomena offered for fiction, he distrusted Spiritualism and believed that the dead had far more worthwhile things to do than send 'messages'. 'Will anyone deny,' he wrote in 'Religion without Dogma?', 'that the vast majority of spirit messages sink pitiably below the best that has been thought and said even in this world? — that in most of them we find a banality and provincialism, a paradoxical union of the prim with the enthusiastic, of flatness and gush, which would suggest that the souls of the moderately respectable are in the keeping of Annie Besant and Martin Tupper?'

Indeed, most of the statements in *The Dark Tower* which touch on the occult come from Orfieu, rather than from Ransom and Lewis who are the only Christians in the story. Lewis had drunk deeply of G. K. Chesterton's works, and when Ransom rejects the notion of reincarnation on the grounds that he is a Christian (p. 29), he is very likely echoing a passage from Lewis's favourite of Chesterton's books, *The Everlasting Man,* which comes as close as anything to explaining why Lewis could not believe in something he found so at variance with Christianity. 'Reincarnation is not really a mystical idea,' said Chesterton. 'It is not really a transcendental idea, or in that sense a religious idea. Mysticism conceives something transcending experience; religion seeks glimpses of a better good or a worse evil than experience can give. Reincarnation need only extend experiences in the sense of repeating them. It is no more transcendental for a man to remember what he did in Babylon before he was born than to remember what he did in Brixton before he had a knock on the head. His successive lives *need* not be any more than human lives, under whatever limitations burden human life. It has nothing to do with seeing God or even conjuring up the devil.' (ch. vi.)

There are, doubtless, others besides myself who were puzzled not to find in the fragment a high theological theme such as that which runs through the other interplanetary books. I think the answer is — indeed Lewis says so himself — that he never began any story with a moral in mind, and that wherever there is one it has pushed its own way in unbidden. Perhaps if he had gone on with *The Dark Tower* such a theme would have emerged, but we cannot be sure. Certainly Lewis does not seem to have known exactly what to do with Ransom who, as far as the story goes, has little of the intellectual and heroic qualities he is abundantly endowed with in *Perelandra, That Hideous Strength* and, to a lesser extent, *Out of the Silent Planet*. All we learn is that he is a kind of 'resident' Christian who has travelled in Deep Heaven. In his 'Reply to Professor Haldane' Lewis says that the Ransom of *That Hideous Strength* (and presumably of *Perelandra* as well) is 'to some extent a fancy portrait of a man I know, but not of me', and Gervase Mathew believes that 'man' is almost certainly Charles Williams, whom Lewis was only just getting to know when he was writing *The Dark Tower*. Gervase Mathew was close to both men, and being in a position to observe Williams' profound influence on Lewis, sees the Ransom of the last two romances as having grown into a kind of idealized Williams – but a Williams, I should venture to guess, underpinned by the steady brilliance and philological genius of Lewis's other great friends, Owen Barfield and J. R. R. Tolkien.

Another point to arise at the Inklings meeting concerned the Stingingman's 'unicorn horn' or 'sting', which Lewis's friends thought suggested unpleasant sexual implications. I do not think Lewis, consciously or unconsciously, intended any such implication. But he took the objection seriously, and I believe this explains why, in chapter 5, when Scudamour begins to grow a 'sting', he bothered to say, 'Of course Scudamour has read his psychoanalysis. He is perfectly well aware that under abnormal conditions a much more natural desire might disguise itself in this grotesque form. But he is pretty sure that this was not what was happening.'

It is teasing to think how Lewis might have continued his story. Weak in mathematics, he may have been unable to imagine a convincing method of extricating Scudamour from the tight place we find him in at the conclusion of the fragment. I am afraid we shall never know what end, or ends (if any), Lewis had in mind for his story before he abandoned it to write a number of other works: *The Problem of Pain* (1940), *The Screwtape Letters* (1942) and *A Preface to Paradise Lost* (1942), which last book possibly gave him the idea for *Perelandra,* which he was working on as early as 1941. It is, besides this, possible, and even likely, that Lewis began other stories the manuscripts of which have not survived. Still, though it was typical of Lewis to be for ever sweeping his manuscripts into his wastepaper-basket, it was unlike him to forget anything.

We have seen how Othertime found its way into other books. There are other elements from *The Dark Tower* which appear, albeit considerably altered, in *That Hideous Strength*. One character who was transferred quite recognizably into the more congenial atmosphere of *That Hideous Strength* is the Scotsman, MacPhee. And it is here that we touch on one of the weak spots in *The Dark Tower*: MacPhee's persistent scepticism about the chronoscope in the face of a month-long daily experience of its actual working. Owen Barfield has said to me about this: 'It's as if Lewis was saying to himself: "I've decided to have an amusing canny Scot as one of my characters and, whatever happens to him, an amusing canny Scot he will jolly well go on being — and *like* it!"'

There are, perhaps, traces of the two Camillas in Jane Studdock of *That Hideous Strength*. Before Lewis changed Camilla's surname to 'Bembridge', which first appears on page 44, she was called Camilla 'Ammeret'. This suggests that the relationship between Scudamour and the two Camillas might have been based on the characters Sir Scudamour and Amoret in Spenser's *Faerie Queene* (book III), where the story is told of how the noble and virtuous Amoret, immediately after her marriage to Sir Scudamour, was carried off by the enchanter Busirane and imprisoned until she was released by Britomart. Lewis may have begun with the idea of a love-affair between his Scudamour and a nice Camilla from Earth, found he needed some reason for transporting Scudamour to Othertime, and then hit on the idea of sending him there to rescue the girl he really loves. Left, then, with an *extra* Camilla, Lewis seems to have decided to make her so 'modern' that she would have been wrong for Scudamour in any case. The character of the Othertime Camilla is never properly developed, but the one on earth tells us a great deal about Lewis's view of the 'liberated' woman and furnishes us with what is possibly the finest little character-study in the book: 'The real Camilla Bembridge . . . was so free to talk about the things her grandmother could not mention that Ransom once said he wondered if she were free to talk about anything else' (p. 76). I think it likely that, by whatever means Scudamour is returned to earth, Lewis would have managed to switch the two women so that the nice one goes home with Scudamour and the 'modern' one ends up in Othertime. One of the books Scudamour is left pondering in Othertime describes how Othertime children had been 'exchanged' for ones from the Earth, and it is not perhaps too fanciful to suppose that Lewis may have thought of having Scudamour discover that the two Camillas had been 'exchanged' when they were children. And perhaps a good many other people as well?

THE MAN BORN BLIND

'Bless us!' said Mary. 'There's eleven o'clock. And you're nearly asleep, Robin.'

She rose with a bustle of familiar noises, bundling her spools and her little cardboard boxes into the work-basket. 'Come on, lazy-bones!' she said. 'You want to be nice and fresh for your first walk tomorrow.'

'That reminds me,' said Robin, and then stopped. His heart was beating so loudly that he was afraid it would make his voice sound odd. He had to wait before he went on. 'I suppose,' he said, 'there . . . there'll be *light* out there – when I go for that walk?'

'What do you mean, dear?' said Mary. 'You mean it will be lighter out of doors? Well, yes, I suppose it will. But I must say I always think this is a very light house. This room, now. We've had the sun on it all day.'

'The sun makes it . . . hot?' said Robin tentatively.

'What *are* you talking about?' said Mary, suddenly turning round. She spoke sharply, in what Robin called her 'governess' voice.

'I mean,' said Robin, '. . . well, look here, Mary. There's a thing I've been meaning to ask you ever since I came back from the nursing home. I know it'll sound silly to you. But then it's different for me. As soon as I knew I had a chance of getting my sight, of course I looked forward. The last thing I thought before the operation was "light". Then all those days afterwards, waiting till they took the bandages off – '

'Of course, darling. That was only natural.'

'Then, then, why don't I . . . I mean, where is the light?'

She laid her hand on his arm. Three weeks of sight had not yet taught him to read the expression of a face, but he knew by her touch the great warm wave of stupid, fright-

99

ened affection that had welled up in her.

'Why not come to bed, Robin dear?' she said. 'If it's anything important, can't we talk about it in the morning? You know you're tired now.'

'No. I've got to have this out. You've got to tell me about light. Great Scot – don't you *want* me to know?'

She sat down suddenly with a formal calmness that alarmed him.

'Very well, Robin,' she said. 'Just ask me anything you like. There's nothing to be worried about – is there?'

'Well then, first of all, there's light in this room at present?'

'Of course there is.'

'Then where is it?'

'Why, all round us.'

'Can you see it?'

'Yes.'

'Then why can't I?'

'But, Robin, you can. Dear, do be sensible. You can see me, can't you, and the mantelpiece, and the table and everything?'

'Are those light? Is that all it means? Are you light? Is the mantelpiece light? Is the table light?'

'Oh! I see. No. Of course not. *That's* the light,' and she pointed to the bulb, roofed with its broad pink shade, that hung from the ceiling.

'If that's light, why did you tell me the light was all round us?'

'I mean, that's what gives the light. The light comes from there.'

'Then where is the light itself? You see, you won't say. Nobody will say. You tell me the light is here and the light is there, and this is in the light and that is in the light, and yesterday you told me I was in *your* light, and now you say that light is a bit of yellow wire in a glass bulb hanging from the ceiling. Call that light? Is that what Milton was talking about? What are you crying about? If you don't know what light is, why can't you say so? If the operation has been a failure and I can't see properly after all, tell me. If there's no such thing – if it was all a fairy tale from the beginning – tell me. But for God's sake – '

'Robin! Robin! Don't. Don't go on like that.'

'Go on like what?' Then he gave it up and apologized and comforted her, and they went to bed.

A blind man has few friends; a blind man who has recently received his sight has, in a sense, none. He belongs neither to the world of the blind nor to that of the seeing, and no one can share his experience. After that night's conversation Robin never mentioned to anyone his problem about light. He knew that he would only be suspected of madness. When Mary took him out next day for his first walk he replied to everything she said, 'It's lovely – all lovely. Just let me drink it in,' and she was satisfied. She interpreted his quick glances as glances of delight. In reality, of course, he was searching, searching with a hunger that had already something of desperation in it. Even had he dared, he knew it would be useless to ask her of any of the objects he saw, 'Is that light?' He could see for himself that she would only answer, 'No. That's green' (or 'blue', or 'yellow', or 'a field', or 'a tree' or 'a car'). Nothing could be done until he had learned to go for walks by himself.

About five weeks later Mary had a headache and took breakfast in bed. As Robin came downstairs he was for a moment shocked to notice the sweet feeling of escape that came with her absence. Then, with a long shameless sigh of comfort, he deliberately closed his eyes and groped across the dining-room to his bookcase – for this one morning he would give up the tedious business of guiding himself by his eyes and judging distances and would enjoy the old, easy methods of the blind. Without effort his fingers ran down the row of faithful Braille books and picked out the worn volume he wanted. He slipped his hand between the leaves and shuffled across to the table, reading as he went. Still with his eyes shut, he cut up his food, laid down the knife, took the fork in his left hand and began reading with his right. He realized at once that this was the first meal he had really enjoyed since the recovery of his sight. It was also the first book he had enjoyed. He had been very quick, everyone told him, in learning to read by sight, but it would never be the real thing. 'W-a-t-e-r' could be spelled out; but never, never would those black marks be wedded to their meaning as in Braille, where the very shape of the characters communicated an instantaneous sense of liquidity through his fingertips. He took a long time over breakfast. Then he went out.

There was a mist that morning, but he had encountered mists before and this did not trouble him. He walked through it, out of the little town and up the steep hill and then along the field path that ran round the lip of the quarry. Mary had taken him there a few days ago to show him what she called the 'view'. And while they had sat looking at it she had said, 'What a lovely light that is on the hills over there.' It was a wretched clue, for he was now convinced that she knew no more about light than he did, that she used the word but meant nothing by it. He was even beginning to suspect that most of the un-blind were in the same position. What one heard among them was merely the parrot-like repetition of a rumour – the rumour of something which perhaps (it was his last hope) great poets and prophets of old had really known and seen. It was on their testimony alone that he still hoped. It was still just possible that somewhere in the world, not everywhere as fools had tried to make him believe, guarded in deep woods or divided by distant seas, the thing Light might actually exist, springing up like a fountain or growing like a flower.

The mist was thinning when he came to the lip of the quarry. To left and right more and more trees were visible and their colours grew brighter every moment. His own shadow lay before him; he noticed that it became blacker and firmer-edged while he looked at it. The birds were singing too and he was quite hot. 'But still no Light', he muttered. The sun was visible behind him but the pit of the quarry was still full of mist – a shapeless whiteness, now almost blindingly white.

Suddenly he heard a man singing. Someone whom he had not noticed before was standing near the cliff edge with his legs wide apart dabbing at an object which Robin could not recognize. If he had been more experienced he would have recognized it as a canvas on an easel. As it was, his eyes met the eyes of this wild-looking stranger so unexpectedly that he had blurted out 'What are you doing?' before he realized it.

'Doing?' said the stranger with a certain savagery. 'Doing? I'm trying to catch light, if you want to know, damn it.'

A smile came over Robin's face. 'So am I,' he said, and came a step nearer.

'Oh – you know too, do you?' said the other. Then, almost vindictively, 'They're all fools. How many of them come out to paint on a day like this, eh? How many of them will recognize it if you show 'em? And yet if they could open their eyes, it's the only sort of day in the whole year when you can really *see* light, solid light, that you could drink in a cup or bathe in! Look at it!'

He caught Robin roughly by the arm and pointed into the depths at their feet. The fog was at death-grips with the sun, but not a stone on the quarry floor was yet visible. The bath of vapour shone like white metal and unfolded itself continually in ever-widening spirals towards them. 'Do you see that?' shouted the violent stranger. 'There's light for you if you like it!'

A second later the expression on the painter's face changed. 'Here!' he cried. 'Are you mad?' He made a grab at Robin. But he was too late. Already he was alone on the path. From beneath a new-made and rapidly vanishing rift in the fog there came up no cry but only a sound so sharp and definite that you would hardly expect it to have been made by the fall of anything so soft as a human body; that, and some rattling of loosened stones.

THE SHODDY LANDS

Being, as I believe, of sound mind and in normal health, I am sitting down at 11 p.m. to record, while the memory of it is still fresh, the curious experience I had this morning.

It happened in my rooms in college, where I am now writing, and began in the most ordinary way with a call on the telephone. 'This is Durward,' the voice said. 'I'm speaking from the porter's lodge. I'm in Oxford for a few hours. Can I come across and see you?' I said yes, of course. Durward is a former pupil and a decent enough fellow; I would be glad to see him again. When he turned up at my door a few moments later I was rather annoyed to find that he had a young woman in tow. I loathe either men or women who speak as if they were coming to see you alone and then spring a husband or a wife, a fiancé or a fiancée on you. One ought to be warned.

The girl was neither very pretty nor very plain, and of course she ruined my conversation. We couldn't talk about any of the things Durward and I had in common because that would have meant leaving her out in the cold. And she and Durward couldn't talk about the things they (presumably) had in common because that would have left me out. He introduced her as 'Peggy' and said they were engaged. After that, the three of us just sat and did social patter about the weather and the news.

I tend to stare when I am bored, and I am afraid I must have stared at that girl, without the least interest, a good deal. At any rate I was certainly doing so at the moment when the strange experience began. Quite suddenly, without any faintness or nausea or anything of that sort, I found myself in a wholly different place. The familiar room vanished; Durward and Peggy vanished. I was alone. And I was standing up.

My first idea was that something had gone wrong with my eyes. I was not in darkness, nor even in twilight, but everything seemed curiously blurred. There was a sort of daylight, but when I looked up I didn't see anything that I could very confidently call a sky. It might, just possibly, be the sky of a very featureless, dull, grey day, but it lacked any suggestion of distance. 'Nondescript' was the word I would have used to describe it. Lower down and closer to me, there were upright shapes, vaguely green in colour, but of a very dingy green. I peered at them for quite a long time before it occurred to me that they might be trees. I went nearer and examined them; and the impression they made on me is not easy to put into words. 'Trees of a sort,' or, 'Well, trees, if you call *that* a tree,' or, 'An attempt at trees,' would come near it. They were the crudest, shabbiest apology for trees you could imagine. They had no real anatomy, no real branches even; they were more like lamp-posts with great, shapeless blobs of green stuck on top of them. Most children could draw better trees from memory.

It was while I was inspecting them that I first noticed the light: a steady, silvery gleam some distance away in the Shoddy Wood. I turned my steps towards it at once, and then first noticed what I was walking on. It was comfortable stuff, soft and cool and springy to the feet; but when you looked down it was horribly disappointing to the eye. It was, in a very rough way, the colour of grass; the colour grass has on a very dull day when you look at it while thinking pretty hard about something else. But there were no separate blades in it. I stooped down and tried to find them; the closer one looked, the vaguer it seemed to become. It had in fact just the same smudged, unfinished quality as the trees : shoddy.

The full astonishment of my adventure was now beginning to descend on me. With it came fear, but, even more, a sort of disgust. I doubt if it can be fully conveyed to anyone who has not had a similar experience. I felt as if I had suddenly been banished from the real, bright, concrete, and prodigally complex world into some sort of second-rate universe that had all been put together on the cheap; by an imitator. But I kept on walking towards the silvery light.

Here and there in the shoddy grass there were patches of what looked, from a distance, like flowers. But each patch, when you came close to it, was as bad as the trees and the grass. You couldn't make out what species they were supposed to be. And they had no real stems or petals; they were mere blobs. As for the colours, I could do better myself with a shilling paint-box.

I should have liked very much to believe that I was dreaming, but somehow I knew I wasn't. My real conviction was that I had died. I wished – with a fervour that no other wish of mine has ever achieved – that I had lived a better life.

A disquieting hypothesis, as you see, was forming in my mind. But next moment it was gloriously blown to bits. Amidst all that shoddiness I came suddenly upon daffodils. Real daffodils, trim and cool and perfect. I bent down and touched them; I straightened my back again and gorged my eyes on their beauty. And not only their beauty but – what mattered to me even more at that moment – their, so to speak, honesty; real, honest, finished daffodils, live things that would bear examination.

But where, then, could I be? 'Let's get on to that light. Perhaps everything will be made clear there. Perhaps it is at the centre of this queer place.'

I reached the light sooner than I expected, but when I reached it I had something else to think about. For now I met the Walking Things. I have to call them that, for 'people' is just what they weren't. They were of human size and they walked on two legs; but they were, for the most part, no more like true men than the Shoddy Trees had been like trees. They were indistinct. Though they were certainly not naked, you couldn't make out what sort of clothes they were wearing, and though there was a pale blob at the top of each, you couldn't say they had faces.

At least that was my first impression. Then I began to notice curious exceptions. Every now and then one of them became partially distinct; a face, a hat, or a dress would stand out in full detail. The odd thing was that the distinct clothes were always women's clothes, but the distinct faces were always those of men. Both facts made the crowd – at least, to a man of my type – about as uninteresting as it could possibly be. The male faces were not the sort I cared about; a flashy-looking crew – gigolos, fripons. But they seemed pleased enough with themselves. Indeed they all wore the same look of fatuous admiration.

I now saw where the light was coming from. I was in a sort of street. At least, behind the crowd of Walking Things on each side, there appeared to be shop-windows, and from these the light came. I thrust my way through the crowd on my left – but my thrusting seemed to yield no physical contacts – and had a look at one of the shops.

Here I had a new surprise. It was a jeweller's, and after the vagueness and general rottenness of most things in that queer place, the sight fairly took my breath away. Everything in that window was perfect; every facet on every diamond distinct, every brooch and tiara finished down to the last perfection of intricate detail. It was good stuff too, as even I could see; there must have been hundreds of thousands of pounds' worth of it. 'Thank Heaven!' I gasped. 'But will it keep on?' Hastily I looked at the next shop. It *was* keeping on. This window contained women's frocks. I'm no judge, so I can't say how good they were. The shop beyond this one sold women's shoes. And it was still keeping on. They were real shoes; the toe-pinching and very high-heeled sort which, to my mind, ruins even the prettiest foot, but at any rate real.

I was just thinking to myself that some people would not find this place half as dull as I did, when the queerness of the whole thing came over me afresh. 'Where the hell,' I began, but immediately changed it to 'Where on earth' – for the other word seemed, in all the circumstances, singularly unfortunate – 'Where on earth have I got to? Trees no good; grass no good; sky no good; flowers no good, except the daffodils; people no good; shops first-class. What can that possibly mean?'

The shops, by the way, were all women's shops, so I soon lost interest in them. I walked the whole length of that street, and then, a little way ahead, I saw sunlight.

Not that it was proper sunlight, of course. There was no break in the dull sky to account for it, no beam slanting down. All that, like so many other things in that world, had not been attended to. There was simply a patch of sunlight on the ground, unexplained, impossible (except that it was there), and therefore not at all cheering; hideous, rather, and disquieting. But I had little time to think about it; for something in the centre of that lighted patch – something I had taken for a small building – suddenly moved, and with a sickening shock I realized that I was looking at a gigantic human shape. It turned round. Its eyes looked straight into mine.

It was not only gigantic, but it was the only complete human shape I had seen since I entered that world. It was female. It was lying on sunlit sand, on a beach apparently, though there was no trace of any sea. It was very nearly naked, but it had a wisp of some brightly coloured stuff round its hips and another round its breasts; like what a modern girl wears on a real beach. The general effect was repulsive, but I saw in a moment or two that this was due to the appalling size. Considered abstractly, the giantess had a good figure; almost a perfect figure, if you like the modern type. The face – but as soon as I had really taken in the face, I shouted out.

'Oh, I say! There you are. Where's Durward? And where's this? What's happened to us?'

But the eyes went on looking straight at me and through me. I was obviously invisible and inaudible to her. But there was no doubt who she was. She was Peggy. That is, she was recognizable; but she was Peggy changed. I don't mean only the size. As regards the figure, it was Peggy improved. I don't think anyone could have denied that. As to the

face, opinions might differ. I would hardly have called the
change an improvement myself. There was no more – I
doubt if there was as much – sense or kindness or honesty
in this face than in the original Peggy's. But it was certainly more regular. The teeth in particular, which I had
noticed as a weak point in the old Peggy, were perfect, as
in a good denture. The lips were fuller. The complexion was
so perfect that it suggested a very expensive doll. The expression I can best describe by saying that Peggy now
looked exactly like the girl in all the advertisements.

If I had to marry either, I should prefer the old, un-
improved Peggy. But even in hell I hoped it wouldn't come
to that.

And, as I watched, the background – the absurd little bit
of sea-beach – began to change. The giantess stood up. She
was on a carpet. Walls and windows and furniture grew
up around her. She was in a bedroom. Even I could tell
it was a very expensive bedroom, though not at all my idea
of good taste. There were plenty of flowers, mostly orchids
and roses, and these were even better finished than the
daffodils had been. One great bouquet (with a card attached
to it) was as good as any I have ever seen. A door which
stood open behind her gave me a view into a bathroom
which I should rather like to own, a bathroom with a sunk
bath. In it there was a French maid fussing about with
towels and bath salts and things. The maid was not nearly
so finished as the roses, or even the towels, but what face
she had looked more French than any real Frenchwoman's
could.

The gigantic Peggy now removed her beach equipment
and stood up naked in front of a full-length mirror. Apparently she enjoyed what she saw there; I can hardly
express how much I didn't. Partly the size (it's only fair
to remember that) but, still more, something that came as
a terrible shock to me, though I suppose modern lovers
and husbands must be hardened to it. Her body was (of
course) brown, like the bodies in the sun-bathing advertisements. But round her hips, and again round her breasts,

where the coverings had been, there were two bands of dead white which looked, by contrast, like leprosy. It made me for the moment almost physically sick. What staggered me was that she could stand and admire it. Had she no idea how it would affect ordinary male eyes? A very disagreeable conviction grew in me that this was a subject of no interest to her; that all her clothes and bath salts and two-piece swimsuits, and indeed the voluptuousness of her every look and gesture, had not, and never had had, the meaning which every man would read, and was intended to read, into them. They were a huge overture to an opera in which she had no interest at all; a coronation procession with no queen at the centre of it; gestures, gestures about nothing.

And now I became aware that two noises had been going for a long time; the only noises I ever heard in that world. But they were coming from outside, from somewhere beyond that low, grey covering which served the Shoddy Lands instead of a sky. Both the noises were knockings – patient knockings, infinitely remote, as if two outsiders, two excluded people, were knocking on the walls of that world. The one was faint, but hard; and with it came a voice saying, 'Peggy, Peggy, let me in.' Durward's voice, I thought. But how shall I describe the other knocking? It was, in some curious way, soft; 'soft as wool and sharp as death', soft but unendurably heavy, as if at each blow some enormous hand fell on the outside of the Shoddy Sky and covered it completely. And with that knocking came a voice at whose sound my bones turned to water : 'Child, child, child, let me in before the night comes.'

'*Before the night comes*' – instantly common daylight rushed back upon me. I was in my own rooms again and my two visitors were before me. They did not appear to notice that anything unusual had happened to me, though, for the rest of that conversation, they might well have supposed I was drunk. I was so happy. Indeed, in a way I was drunk – drunk with the sheer delight of being back in the real world, free, outside the horrible little prison of that land.

There were birds singing close to a window; there was real sunlight falling on a panel. That panel needed repainting; but I could have gone down on my knees and kissed its very shabbiness – the precious real, solid, thing it was. I noticed a tiny cut on Durward's cheek where he must have cut himself shaving that morning; and I felt the same about it. Indeed anything was enough to make me happy : I mean, any Thing, as long as it really was a Thing.

Well, those are the facts; everyone may make what he pleases of them. My own hypothesis is the obvious one which will have occurred to most readers. It may be too obvious; I am quite ready to consider rival theories. My view is that by the operation of some unknown psychological – or pathological law, I was, for a second or so, let into Peggy's mind; at least to the extent of seeing her world, the world as it exists for her. At the centre of that world is a swollen image of herself, remodelled to be as like the girls in the advertisements as possible. Round this are grouped clear and distinct images of the things she really cares about. Beyond that, the whole earth and sky are a vague blur. The daffodils and roses are especially instructive. Flowers only exist for her if they are the sort that can be cut and put in vases or sent as bouquets; flowers in themselves, flowers as you see them in the woods, are negligible.

As I say, this is probably not the only hypothesis which will fit the facts. But it has been a most disquieting experience. Not only because I am sorry for poor Durward. Suppose this sort of thing were to become common? And how if, some other time, I were not the explorer but the explored?

MINISTERING ANGELS

The Monk, as they called him, settled himself on the camp-chair beside his bunk and stared through the window at the harsh sand and black-blue sky of Mars. He did not mean to begin his 'work' for ten minutes yet. Not, of course, the work he had been brought there to do. He was the meteorologist of the party, and his work in that capacity was largely done; he had found out whatever could be found out. There was nothing more, within the limited radius he could investigate, to be observed for at least twenty-five days. And meteorology had not been his real motive. He had chosen three years on Mars as the nearest modern equivalent to a hermitage in the desert. He had come there to meditate: to continue the slow, perpetual re-building of that inner structure which, in his view, it was the main purpose of life to rebuild. And now his ten minutes' rest was over. He began with his well-used formula. 'Gentle and patient Master, teach me to need men less and to love thee more.' Then to it. There was no time to waste. There were barely six months of this lifeless, sinless, un-suffering wilderness ahead of him. Three years were short – but when the shout came he rose out of his chair with the practised alertness of a sailor.

The Botanist in the next cabin responded to the same shout with a curse. His eye had been at the microscope when it came. It was maddening. Constant interruption. A man might as well try to work in the middle of Piccadilly as in this infernal camp. And his work was already a race against time. Six months more – and he had hardly begun. The flora of Mars, these tiny, miraculously hardy organisms, the ingenuity of their contrivances to live under all but impossible conditions – it was a feast for a lifetime. He would ignore the shout. But then came the bell. All hands to the main room.

The only person who was doing, so to speak, nothing when the shout came was the Captain. To be more exact, he was (as usual) trying to stop thinking about Clare, and get on with his official journal. Clare kept on interrupting from forty million miles away. It was preposterous. '*Would have needed all hands,*' he wrote. Hands . . . his own hands . . . his own hands, hands, he felt, with eyes in them, travelling over all the warm-cool, soft-firm, smooth, yielding, resisting aliveness of her. 'Shut up, there's a dear,' he said to the photo on his desk. And so back to the journal, until the fatal words '*had been causing me some anxiety*'. Anxiety— oh God, what might be happening to Clare now? How did he know there was a Clare by this time? Anything could happen. He'd been a fool ever to accept this job. What other newly married man in the world would have done it? But it had seemed so sensible. Three years of horrid separation but then . . . oh, they were made for life. He had been promised the post that, only a few months before, he would not have dared to dream of. He'd never need to go to Space again. And all the by-products; the lectures, the book, probably a title. Plenty of children. He knew she wanted that, and so in a queer way (as he began to find) did he. But damn it, the journal. Begin a new paragraph— and then the shout came.

It was one of the two youngsters, technicians both, who had given it. They had been together since dinner. At least Paterson had been standing at the open door of Dickson's cabin, shifting from foot to foot and swinging the door, and Dickson had been sitting on his berth and waiting for Paterson to go away.

'What are you talking about, Paterson?' he said. 'Who ever said anything about a quarrel?'

'That's all very well, Bobby,' said the other, 'but we're not friends like we used to be. You know we're not. Oh, *I'm* not blind. I *did* ask you to call me Clifford. And you're always so stand-offish.'

'Oh, get to hell out of this!' cried Dickson. 'I'm perfectly ready to be good friends with you and everyone else in an ordinary way, but all this gas – like a pair of school-girls – I will not stand. Once and for all – '

'Oh look, look, look,' said Paterson. And it was then that Dickson shouted and the Captain came and rang the bell and within twenty seconds they were all crowded behind the biggest of the windows. A spaceship had just made a beautiful landing about a hundred and fifty yards from camp.

'Oh boy!' exclaimed Dickson. 'They're relieving us before our time.'

'Damn their eyes. Just what they would do,' said the Botanist.

Five figures were descending from the ship. Even in space-suits it was clear that one of them was enormously fat; they were in no other way remarkable.

'Man the air-lock,' said the Captain.

Drinks from their limited store were going round. The Captain had recognized in the leader of the strangers an old acquaintance, Ferguson. Two were ordinary young men, not unpleasant. But the remaining two?

'I don't understand,' said the Captain, 'who exactly – I mean we're delighted to see you all of course – but what exactly . . . ?'

'Where are the rest of your party?' said Ferguson.

'We've had two casualties, I'm afraid,' said the Captain. 'Sackville and Dr Burton. It was a most wretched business. Sackville tried eating the stuff we called Martian cress. It drove him fighting mad in a matter of minutes. He knocked Burton down and by sheer bad luck Burton fell in just the wrong position: across that table there. Broke his neck. We got Sackville tied down on a bunk but he was dead before the evening.'

'Hadna he even the gumption to try it on the guinea-pig first?' said Ferguson.

'Yes,' said the Botanist. 'That was the whole trouble. The funny thing is that the guinea-pig lived. But its be-haviour was remarkable. Sackville wrongly concluded that the stuff was alcoholic. Thought he'd invent a new drink. The nuisance is that once Burton was dead, none of us could do a reliable post-mortem on Sackville. Under analysis this vegetable shows – '

'A-a-a-h,' interrupted one of those who had not yet spoken. 'We must beware of oversimplifications. I doubt if the vegetable substance is the real explanation. There are stresses and strains. You are all, without knowing it, in a highly unstable condition, for reasons which are no mystery to a trained psychologist.'

Some of those present had doubted the sex of this creature. Its hair was very short, its nose very long, its mouth very prim, its chin sharp, and its manner authoritative. The voice revealed it as, scientifically speaking, a woman. But no one had had any doubt about the sex of her nearest neighbour, the fat person.

'Oh dearie,' she wheezed. 'Not now. I tell you straight I'm that flustered and faint, I'll scream if you go on so. Suppose there ain't such a thing as a port and lemon handy? No? Well, a little drop more gin would settle me. It's me stomach reelly.'

The speaker was infinitely female and perhaps in her seventies. Her hair had been not very successfully dyed to a colour not unlike that of mustard. The powder (scented strongly enough to throw a train off the rails) lay like snow drifts in the complex valleys of her creased, many-chinned face.

'Stop!' roared Ferguson. 'Whatever ye do, dinna give her a drap mair to drink.'

"'E's no 'art, ye see,' said the old woman with a whimper and an affectionate leer directed at Dickson.

'Excuse me,' said the Captain. 'Who are these – ah – ladies and what is this all about?'

'I have been waiting to explain,' said the Thin Woman, and cleared her throat. 'Anyone who has been following World-Opinion-Trends on the problems arising out of the psychological welfare aspect of interplanetary communication will be conscious of the growing agreement that such a remarkable advance inevitably demands of us far-reaching ideological adjustments. Psychologists are now well aware that a forcible inhibition of powerful biological urges over a protracted period is likely to have unforeseeable results. The pioneers of space-travel are exposed to this danger. It would be unenlightened if a supposed ethicality were allowed to stand in the way of their protection. We must therefore nerve ourselves to face the view that immorality, as it has hitherto been called, must no longer be regarded as unethical – '

'I don't understand that,' said the Monk.

'She means,' said the Captain, who was a good linguist, 'that what you call fornication must no longer be regarded as immoral.'

'That's right, dearie,' said the Fat Woman to Dickson, 'she only means a poor boy needs a woman now and then. It's only natural.'

'What was required, therefore,' continued the Thin Woman, 'was a band of devoted females who would take the first step. This would expose them, no doubt, to obloquy from many ignorant persons. They would be sustained by the consciousness that they were performing an indispensable function in the history of human progress.'

'She means you're to have tarts, duckie,' said the Fat Woman to Dickson.

'Now you're talking,' said he with enthusiasm. 'Bit late in the day, but better late than never. But you can't have brought many girls in that ship. And why didn't you bring them in? Or are they following?'

'We cannot indeed claim,' continued the Thin Woman, who had apparently not noticed the interruption, 'that the response to our appeal was such as we had hoped. The personnel of the first unit of the Woman's Higher Aphro-disio-Therapeutic Humane Organization (abbreviated WHAT-HO) is not perhaps . . . well. Many excellent women, university colleagues of my own, even senior colleagues, to whom I applied, showed themselves curiously conventional. But at least a start has been made. And here,' she concluded brightly, 'we are.'

And there, for forty seconds of appalling silence, they were. Then Dickson's face, which had already undergone certain contortions, became very red; he applied his handkerchief and spluttered like a man trying to stifle a sneeze, rose abruptly, turned his back on the company, and hid his face. He stood slightly stooped and you could see his shoulders shaking.

Paterson jumped up and ran towards him; but the Fat Woman, though with infinite gruntings and upheavals, had risen too.

'Get art of it, Pansy,' she snarled at Paterson. 'Lot o' good your sort ever did.' A moment later her vast arms were round Dickson; all the warm, wobbling maternalism of her engulfed him.

'There, sonny,' she said, 'it's goin' to be OK. Don't cry, honey. Don't cry. Poor boy, then. Poor boy. I'll give you a good time.'

'I think,' said the Captain, 'the young man is laughing, not crying.'

It was the Monk who at this point mildly suggested a meal.

Some hours later the party had temporarily broken up.

Dickson (despite all his efforts the Fat Woman had contrived to sit next to him; she had more than once mistaken his glass for hers) had hardly finished his last mouthful when he said to the newly arrived technicians:

'I'd love to see over your ship, if I could.'

You might expect that two men who had been cooped up in that ship so long, and had only taken off their spacesuits a few minutes ago, would have been reluctant to reassume the one and return to the other. That was certainly the Fat Woman's view. 'Nar, nar,' she said. 'Don't you go fidgeting, sonny. They seen enough of that ruddy ship for a bit, same as me. 'Tain't good for you to go rushing about, not on a full stomach, like.' But the two young men were marvellously obliging.

'Certainly. Just what I was going to suggest,' said the first. 'OK by me, chum,' said the second. They were all three of them out of the air-lock in record time.

Across the sand, up the ladder, helmets off, and then:

'What in the name of thunder have you dumped those two bitches on us for?' said Dickson.

'Don't fancy 'em?' said the Cockney stranger. 'The people at 'ome thought as 'ow you'd be a bit sharp set by now. Ungrateful of you, I call it.'

'Very funny to be sure,' said Dickson. 'But it's no laughing matter for us.'

'It hasn't been for us either, you know,' said the Oxford stranger. 'Cheek by jowl with them for eighty-five days. They palled a bit after the first month.'

'You're telling me,' said the Cockney.

There was a disgusted pause.

'Can anyone tell me,' said Dickson at last, 'who in the world, and why in the world, out of all possible women, selected those two horrors to send to Mars?'

'Can't expect a star London show at the back of beyond,' said the Cockney.

'My dear fellow,' said his colleague, 'isn't the thing perfectly obvious? What kind of woman, without force, is going to come and live in this ghastly place – on rations – and play doxy to half a dozen men she's never seen? The Good Time Girls won't come because they know you can't have a good time on Mars. An ordinary professional prostitute won't come as long as she has the slightest chance of being picked up in the cheapest quarter of Liverpool or Los Angeles. And you've got one who hasn't. The only other who'd come would be a crank who believes all that blah about the new ethicality. And you've got one of that too.'

'Simple, ain't it?' said the Cockney.

'Anyone,' said the other, 'except the Fools at the Top could of course have foreseen it from the word go.'

'The only hope now is the Captain,' said Dickson.

'Look, mate,' said the Cockney, 'if you think there's

any question of our taking back returned goods, you've 'ad it. Nothing doing. Our Captain'll 'ave a mutiny to settle if he tries that. Also 'e won't. 'E's 'ad 'is turn. So've we. It's up to you now.'

'Fair's fair, you know,' said the other. 'We've stood all we can.'

'Well,' said Dickson, 'we must leave the two chiefs to fight it out. But discipline or not, there are some things a man can't stand. That bloody schoolmarm —'

'She's a lecturer at a redbrick university, actually.'

'Well,' said Dickson after a long pause, 'you were going to show me over the ship. It might take my mind off it a bit.'

The Fat Woman was talking to the Monk. '. . . and oh, Father dear, I know you'll think that's the worst of all. I didn't give it up when I could. After me brother's wife died . . . 'e'd 'ave 'ad me 'ome with 'im, and money wasn't that short. But I went on, Gawd 'elp me, I went on.'

'Why did you do that, daughter?' said the Monk. 'Did you *like* it?'

'Well not all that, Father. I was never partikler. But you see — oh, Father, I was the goods in those days, though you wouldn't think it now . . . and the poor gentlemen, they did so enjoy it.'

'Daughter,' he said, 'you are not far from the Kingdom. But you were wrong. The desire to give is blessed. But you can't turn bad bank-notes into good ones just by giving them away.'

The Captain had also left the table pretty quickly, asking Ferguson to accompany him to his cabin. The Botanist had leaped after them.

'One moment, sir, one moment,' he said excitedly. 'I am a scientist. I'm working at very high pressure already. I hope there is no complaint to be made about my discharge of all those other duties which so incessantly interrupt my work. But if I am going to be expected to waste any more time entertaining those abominable females – '

'When I give you any orders which can be considered *ultra vires*,' said the Captain, 'it will be time to make your protest.'

Paterson stayed with the Thin Woman. The only part of any woman that interested him was her ears. He liked telling women about his troubles; especially about the unfairness and unkindness of other men. Unfortunately the lady's idea was that the interview should be devoted either to Aphrodisio-Therapy or to instruction in psychology. She saw, indeed, no reason why the two operations should not be carried out simultaneously; it is only untrained minds that cannot hold more than one idea. The difference between these two conceptions of the conversation was well on its way to impairing its success. Paterson was becoming ill-tempered; the lady remained bright and patient as an iceberg.

'But as I was saying,' grumbled Paterson, 'what I do think so rotten is a fellow being quite fairly decent one day and then – '

'Which just illustrates my point. These tensions and maladjustments are bound, under the unnatural conditions, to arise. And provided we disinfect the obvious remedy of all those sentimental or – which is quite as bad – prurient associations which the Victorian age attached to it – '

'But I haven't yet told you. Listen. Only two days ago – '

'One moment. This ought to be regarded like any other injection. If once we can persuade – '

'How any fellow can take a pleasure – '

'I agree. The association of it with pleasure (that is purely an adolescent fixation) may have done incalculable harm. Rationally viewed – '

'I say, you're getting off the point.'

'One moment – '

The dialogue continued.

They had finished looking over the spaceship. It was certainly a beauty. No one afterwards remembered who had first said, 'Anyone could manage a ship like this.'

Ferguson sat quietly smoking while the Captain read the letter he had brought him. He didn't even look in the Captain's direction. When at last conversation began there was so much circumambient happiness in the cabin that they took a long time to get down to the difficult part of their business. The Captain seemed at first wholly occupied with its comic side.

'Still,' he said at last, 'it has its serious side too. The impertinence of it, for one thing! Do they think – '

'Ye maun recall,' said Ferguson, 'they're dealing with an absolutely new situation.'

'Oh, *new* be damned! How does it differ from men on whalers, or even on windjammers in the old days? Or on the North-west Frontier? It's about as new as people being hungry when food was short.'

'Eh mon, but ye're forgettin' the new light of modern psychology.'

'I think those two ghastly women have already learned some newer psychology since they arrived. Do they really suppose every man in the world is so combustible that he'll jump into the arms of any woman whatever?'

'Aye, they do. They'll be sayin' you and your party are verra abnormal. I wadna put it past them to be sending you out wee packets of hormones next.'

'Well, if it comes to that, do they suppose men would volunteer for a job like this unless they could, or thought they could, or wanted to try if they could, do without women?'

'Then there's the new ethics, forbye.'

'Oh stow it, you old rascal. What is new there either? Who ever tried to live clean except a minority who had a religion or were in love? They'll try it still on Mars, as they did on Earth. As for the majority, did they ever hesitate to take their pleasures wherever they could get them? The ladies of the profession know better. Did you ever see a port or a garrison town without plenty of brothels?

Who are the idiots on the Advisory Council who started all this nonsense?'

'Och, a pack o' daft auld women (in trousers for the maist part) who like onything sexy, and onything scientific, and onything that makes them feel important. And this gives them all three pleasures at once, ye ken.'

'Well, there's only one thing for it, Ferguson. I'm not going to have either your Mistress Overdone or your extension lecturer here. You can just – '

'Now there's no manner of use talkin' that way. I did my job. Another voyage with sic a cargo o' livestock I will not face. And my two lads the same. There'd be mutiny and murder.'

'But you must, I'm – '

At that moment a blinding flash came from without and the earth shook.

'Ma ship! Ma ship!' cried Ferguson. Both men peered out on empty sand. The spaceship had obviously made an excellent take-off.

'But what's happened?' said the Captain. 'They haven't – '

'Mutiny, desertion, and theft of a government ship, that's what's happened,' said Ferguson. 'Ma twa lads and your Dickson are awa' hame.'

'But good Lord, they'll get hell for this. They've ruined their careers. They'll be – '

'Aye. Nae dout. And they think it cheap at the price. Ye'll be seeing why, maybe, before ye are a fortnight older.'

A gleam of hope came into the Captain's eyes. 'They couldn't have taken the women with them?'

'Talk sense, mon, talk sense. Or if ye hanna ony sense, use your ears.'

In the buzz of excited conversation which became every moment more audible from the main room, female voices could be intolerably distinguished.

As he composed himself for his evening meditation the Monk thought that perhaps he had been concentrating too much on 'needing less' and that must be why he was going to have a course (advanced) in 'loving more'. Then his face twitched into a smile that was not all mirth. He was thinking of the Fat Woman. Four things made an exquisite chord. First, the horror of all she had done and suffered. Secondly, the pity – thirdly, the comicality – of her belief that she could still excite desire; fourthly, her bless'd ignorance of that utterly different loveliness which already existed within her and which, under grace, and with such poor direction as even he could supply, might one day set her, bright in the land of brightness, beside the Magdalene.

But wait! There was yet a fifth note in the chord. 'Oh, Master,' he murmured, 'forgive – or can you enjoy? – my absurdity also. I had been supposing you sent me on a voyage of forty million miles merely for my own spiritual convenience.'

FORMS OF THINGS
UNKNOWN

'... that what was myth in one world might always be fact in some other.' PERELANDRA

'Before the class breaks up, gentlemen,' said the instructor, 'I should like to make some reference to a fact which is known to some of you, but probably not yet to all. High Command, I need not remind you, has asked for a volunteer for yet one more attempt on the Moon. It will be the fourth. You know the history of the previous three. In each case the explorers landed unhurt; or at any rate alive. We got their messages. Every message short, some apparently interrupted. And after that never a word, gentlemen. I think the man who offers to make the fourth voyage has about as much courage as anyone I've heard of. And I can't tell you how proud it makes me that he is one of my own pupils. He is in this room at this moment. We wish him every possible good fortune. Gentlemen, I ask you to give three cheers for Lieutenant John Jenkin.'

Then the class became a cheering crowd for two minutes; after that a hurrying, talkative crowd in the corridor. The two biggest cowards exchanged the various family reasons which had deterred them from volunteering themselves. The knowing man said, 'There's something behind all this.' The vermin said, 'He always was a chap who'd do anything to get himself into the limelight.' But most just shouted out, 'Jolly good show, Jenkin,' and wished him luck.

Ward and Jenkin got away together into a pub.

'You kept this pretty dark,' said Ward. 'What's yours?'

'A pint of draught Bass,' said Jenkin.

'Do you want to talk about it?' said Ward rather awkwardly when the drinks had come. 'I mean – if you won't think I'm butting in – it's not just because of that girl, is it?'

'That girl' was a young woman who was thought to have treated Jenkin rather badly.

'Well,' said Jenkin, 'I don't suppose I'd be going if she had married me. But it's not a spectacular attempt at suicide or any rot of that sort. I'm not depressed. I don't feel anything particular about her. Not much interested in women at all, to tell you the truth. Not now. A bit petrified.'

'What is it then?'

'Sheer unbearable curiosity. I've read those three little messages over and over till I know them by heart. I've heard every theory there is about what interrupted them. I've –'

'Is it certain they were all interrupted? I thought one of them was supposed to be complete.'

'You mean Traill and Henderson? I think it was as incomplete as the others. First there was Stafford. He went alone, like me.'

'Must you? I'll come, if you'll have me.'

Jenkin shook his head. 'I knew you would,' he said. 'But you'll see in a moment why I don't want you to. But to go back to the messages. Stafford's was obviously cut short by something. It went: "Stafford from within fifty miles of Point X0308 on the Moon. My landing was excellent. I have –" then silence. Then come Traill and Henderson. "We have landed. We are perfectly well. The ridge M392 is straight ahead of me as I speak. Over."'

'What do you make of "Over"?'

'Not what you do. You think it means "finis" – the message is over. But who in the world, speaking to Earth from the Moon for the first time in all history, would have so little to say – if he *could* say any more? As if he'd crossed to Calais and sent his grandmother a card to say "Arrived safely". The thing's ludicrous.'

'Well, what do *you* make of "Over"?'

'Wait a moment. The last lot were Trevor, Woodford, and Fox. It was Fox who sent the message. Remember it?'

'Probably not so accurately as you.'

'Well, it was this. "This is Fox speaking. All has gone wonderfully well. A perfect landing. You shot pretty well for I'm on Point X0308 at this moment. Ridge M392 straight ahead. On my left, far away across the crater, I see the big peaks. On my right I see the Yerkes cleft. Behind me." Got it?'

'I don't see the point.'

'Well, Fox was cut off the moment he said "Behind me". Supposing Traill was cut off in the middle of saying "Over my shoulder I can see" or "Over behind me", or something like that?'

'You mean –'

'All the evidence is consistent with the view that everything went well till the speaker looked behind him. Then something got him.'

'What sort of something?'

'That's what I want to find out. One idea in my head is this. Might there be something on the Moon – or something psychological about the experience of landing on the Moon – which drives men fighting mad?'

'I see. You mean Fox looked round just in time to see Trevor and Woodford preparing to knock him on the head?'

'Exactly. And Traill – for it was Traill – just in time to see Henderson a split second before Henderson murdered him. And that's why I'm not going to risk having a companion; least of all my best friend.'

'This doesn't explain Stafford.'

'No. That's why one can't rule out the other hypothesis.'

'What's it?'

'Oh, that whatever killed them all was something they found there. Something lunar.'

'You're surely not going to suggest life on the Moon at this time of day?'

'The word "life" always begs the question. Because, of course, it suggests organization as we know it on Earth – with all the chemistry which organization involves. Of course there could hardly be anything of that sort. But there might – I at any rate can't say there couldn't – be masses of matter capable of movements determined from within, determined, in fact, by intentions.'

'Oh Lord, Jenkin, that's nonsense. Animated stones, no doubt! That's mere science fiction or mythology.'

'Going to the Moon at all was once science fiction. And as for mythology, haven't they found the Cretan labyrinth?'

'And all it really comes down to,' said Ward, 'is that no one has ever come back from the Moon, and no one, so far as we know, ever survived there for more than a few minutes. Damn the whole thing.' He stared gloomily into his tankard.

'Well,' said Jenkin cheerily, 'somebody's got to go. The whole human race isn't going to be licked by any blasted satellite.'

'I might have known that was your real reason,' said Ward.

'Have another pint and don't look so glum,' said Jenkin. 'Anyway, there's loads of time. I don't suppose they'll get me off for another six months at the earliest.'

But there was hardly any time. Like any man in the modern world on whom tragedy has descended or who has undertaken a high enterprise, he lived for the next few months a life not unlike that of a hunted animal. The Press, with all their cameras and notebooks, were after him. They did not care in the least whether he was allowed to eat or sleep or whether they made a nervous wreck of him before he took off. 'Flesh-flies,' he called them. When forced to address them, he always said, 'I wish I could take you all with me.' But he reflected also that a Saturn's ring of dead (and burnt) reporters circling round his spaceship might get on his nerves. They would hardly make 'the silence of those eternal spaces' any more homelike.

The take-off when it came was a relief. But the voyage was worse than he had ever anticipated. Not physically – on that side it was nothing worse than uncomfortable – but in the emotional experience. He had dreamed all his life, with mingled terror and longing, of those eternal spaces; of being utterly 'outside', in the sky. He had wondered if the agoraphobia of that roofless and bottomless vacuity would overthrow his reason. But the moment he had been shut into his ship there descended upon him the suffocating knowledge that the real danger of space-travel is claustrophobia. You have been put in a little metal container; somewhat like a cupboard, very like a coffin. You can't see out; you can see things only on the screen. Space and the stars are just as remote as they were on the Earth. Where you are is always your world. The sky is never where you are. All you have done is to exchange a large world of earth and rock and water and clouds for a tiny world of metal.

This frustration of a life-long desire bit deeply into his mind as the cramped hours passed. Then he became conscious of another motive which, unnoticed, had been at work on him when he volunteered. That affair with the girl had indeed frozen him stiff; petrified him, you might say. He wanted to feel again, to be flesh, not stone. To feel anything, even terror. Well, on this trip there would be terrors enough before all was done. He'd be wakened, never fear. That part of his destiny at least he felt he could shake off.

The landing was not without terror, but there were so many gimmicks to look after, so much skill to be exercised, that it did not amount to very much. But his heart was beating a little more noticeably than usual as he put the finishing touches to his space-suit and climbed out. He was carrying the transmission apparatus with him. It felt, as he had expected, as light as a loaf. But he was not going to send any message in a hurry. That might be where all the others had gone wrong. Anyway, the longer he waited the longer those pressmen would be kept out of their beds waiting for their story. Do 'em good.

The first thing that struck him was that his helmet had been too lightly tinted. It was painful to look at all in the direction of the sun. Even the rock – it was, after all, rock not dust (which disposed of one hypothesis) – was dazzling. He put down the apparatus; tried to take in the scene.

The surprising thing was how small it looked. He thought he could account for this. The lack of atmosphere forbade nearly all the effect that distance has on Earth. The serrated boundary of the crater was, he knew, about twenty-five miles away. It looked as if you could have touched it. The peaks looked as if they were a few feet high. The black sky, with its inconceivable multitude and ferocity of stars, was like a cap forced down upon the crater; the stars only just out of his reach. The impression of a stage-set in a toy theatre, therefore of something arranged, therefore of something waiting for him, was at once disappointing and oppressive. Whatever terrors there might be, here too agoraphobia would not be one of them.

He took his bearings and the result was easy enough. He was, like Fox and his friends, almost exactly on Point X0308. But there was no trace of human remains.

If he could find any, he might have some clue as to how they died. He began to hunt. He went in each circle further from the ship. There was no danger of losing it in a place like this.

Then he got his first real shock of fear. Worse still, he could not tell what was frightening him. He only knew that he was engulfed in sickening unreality; seemed neither to be where he was nor to be doing what he did. It was also somehow connected with an experience long ago. It was something that had happened in a cave. Yes; he remembered now. He had been walking along supposing himself alone and then noticed that there was always a sound of other feet following him. Then in a flash he realized what was wrong. This was the exact reverse of the experience in the cave. Then there had been too many footfalls. Now there were too few. He walked on hard rock as silently as a ghost. He swore at himself for a fool – as if every child didn't know that a world without air would be a world without noise. But the silence, though explained, became none the less terrifying.

He had now been alone on the Moon for perhaps thirty-five minutes. It was then that he noticed the three strange things.

The sun's rays were roughly at right angles to his line of sight, so that each of the things had a bright side and a dark side; for each dark side a shadow like Indian ink lay out on the rock. He thought they looked like Belisha beacons. Then he thought they looked like huge apes. They were about the height of a man. They were indeed like clumsily shaped men. Except – he resisted an impulse to vomit – that they had no heads.

They had something instead. They were (roughly) human up to their shoulders. Then, where the head should have been, there was utter monstrosity – a huge spherical block; opaque, featureless. And every one of them looked as if it had that moment stopped moving or were at that moment about to move.

Ward's phrase about 'animated stones' darted up hideously from his memory. And hadn't he himself talked of something that we couldn't call life, not in our sense, something that could nevertheless produce locomotion and have intentions? Something which, at any rate, shared with life life's tendency to kill? If there were such creatures – mineral equivalents to organisms – they could probably stand perfectly still for a hundred years without feeling any strain.

Were they aware of him? What had they for senses? The opaque globes on their shoulders gave no hint.

There comes a moment in nightmare, or sometimes in real battle, when fear and courage both dictate the same course : to rush, planless, upon the thing you are afraid of. Jenkin sprang upon the nearest of the three abominations and rapped his gloved knuckles against it globular top.

Ach ! – he'd forgotten. No noise. All the bombs in the world might burst here and make no noise. Ears are useless on the Moon.

He recoiled a step and next moment found himself sprawling on the ground. 'This is how they all died,' he thought.

But he was wrong. The figure above him had not stirred. He was quite undamaged. He got up again and saw what he had tripped over.

It was a purely terrestrial object. It was, in fact, a transmission set. Not exactly like his own, but an earlier and supposedly inferior model – the sort Fox would have had.

As the truth dawned on him an excitement very different from that of terror seized him. He looked at their misshaped bodies; then down at his own limbs. Of course; that was what one looked like in a space-suit. On his own head there was a similar monstrous globe, but fortunately not an opaque one. He was looking at three statues of spacemen: at statues of Trevor, Woodford, and Fox.

But then the Moon must have inhabitants; and rational inhabitants; more than that, artists.

And what artists! You might quarrel with their taste, for no line anywhere in any of the three statues had any beauty. You could not say a word against their skill. Except for the head and face inside each headpiece, which obviously could not be attempted in such a medium, they were perfect. Photographic accuracy had never reached such a point on earth. And though they were faceless you could see from the set of their shoulders, and indeed of their whole bodies, that a momentary pose had been exactly seized. Each was the statue of a man turning to look behind him. Months of work had doubtless gone to the carving of each; it caught that instantaneous gesture like a stone snapshot.

Jenkin's idea was now to send his message at once. Before anything happened to himself, Earth must hear this amazing news. He set off in great strides, and presently in leaps – now first enjoying lunar gravitation – for his ship and his own set. He was happy now. He *had* escaped his destiny. Petrified, eh? No more feelings? Feelings enough to last him for ever.

He fixed the set so that he could stand with his back to the sun. He worked the gimmicks. 'Jenkin, speaking from the Moon,' he began.

His own huge black shadow lay out before him. There is no noise on the Moon. Up from behind the shoulders of his own shadow another shadow pushed its way along the dazzling rock. It was that of a human head. And what a head of hair. It was all rising, writhing – swaying in the wind perhaps. Very thick the hairs looked. Then, as he turned in terror, there flashed through his mind the thought, 'But there's no wind. No air. It can't be *blowing* about.' His eyes met hers.

AFTER TEN YEARS

I

For several minutes now Yellowhead had thought seriously
of moving his right leg. Though the discomfort of his present
position was almost unbearable, the move was not lightly
to be undertaken. Not in this darkness, packed so close
as they were. The man next to him (he could not remember
who it was) might be asleep or might at least be tolerably
comfortable, so that he would growl or even curse if you
pressed or pushed him. A quarrel would be fatal; and some
of the company were hot-tempered and loud-voiced enough.
There were other things to avoid too. The place stank vilely;
they had been shut up for hours with all their natural neces-
sities (fears included) upon them. Some of them – skeery
young fools – had vomited. But that had been when the
whole thing moved, so there was some excuse; they had
been rolled to and fro in their prison, left, right, up and
(endlessly, sickeningly) down; worse than a storm at sea.

That had been hours ago. He wondered how many
hours. It must be evening by now. The light which, at first,
had come down to them through the sloping shaft at one
end of the accursed contraption had long ago disappeared.
They were in perfect blackness. The humming of insects
had stopped. The stale air was beginning to be chilly. It
must be well after sunset.

Cautiously he tried to extend his leg. It met at once hard
muscle; defiantly hard muscle in the leg of someone who
was wide awake and wouldn't budge. So that line was no
good. Yellowhead drew back his foot further and brought
his knee up under his chin. It was not a position you could
hold for long, but for a moment it was relief. Oh, if once
they were out of this thing . . .

And when they were, what next? Plenty of chance to
get the fidgets out of one's limbs then. There might be
two hours of pretty hard work; not more, he thought. That

is, if everything went well. And after that? After that, he would find the Wicked Woman. He was sure he would find her. It was known that she had been still alive within the last month. He'd get her all right. And he would do such things to her . . . Perhaps he would torture her. He told himself, but all in words, about the tortures. He had to do it in words because no pictures of it would come into his mind. Perhaps he'd have her first; brutally, insolently, like an enemy and a conqueror; show her she was no more than any other captured girl. And she was no more than any girl. The pretence that she was somehow different, the endless flattery, was most likely what had sent her wrong to begin with. People were such fools.

Perhaps, when he had had her himself, he'd give her to the other prisoners to make sport for them. Excellent. But he'd pay the slaves out for touching her too. The picture of what he'd do to the slaves formed itself quite easily.

He had to extend his leg again, but now he found that the place where it had lain had somehow filled itself up. That other man had overflowed into it and Yellowhead was the worse off for his move. He twisted himself round a little so as to rest partly on his left hip. This too was something he had to thank the Wicked Woman for; it was on her account that they were all smothering in this den.

But he wouldn't torture her. He saw that was nonsense. Torture was all very well for getting information; it was no real use for revenge. All people under torture have the same face and make the same noise. You lose the person you hated. And it never makes them feel wicked. And she was young; only a girl. He could pity her. There were tears in his eyes. Perhaps it would be better just to kill her. No rape, no punishments; just a solemn, stately, mournful, almost regretful killing, like a sacrifice.

But they had to get out first. The signal from outside ought to have come hours ago. Perhaps all the others, all round him in the dark, were quite certain that something had gone wrong, and each was waiting for someone else to say it. There was no difficulty in thinking of things that might have gone wrong. He saw now that the whole plan had been crazy from the beginning. What was there to prevent their all being roasted alive where they sat? Why should their own friends from outside ever find them? Or find them alone and unguarded? How if no signal ever came and they never got out at all? They were in a death-trap.

He dug his nails into his palms and shut off these thoughts by mere force. For everyone knew, and everyone had said before they got in, that these were the very thoughts that would come during the long wait, and that at all costs you must not think them; whatever else you pleased, but not those.

He started thinking about the Woman again. He let pictures rise in the dark, all kinds; clothed, naked, asleep, awake, drinking, dancing, nursing the child, laughing. A little spark of desire began to glow; the old, ever-renewed astonishment. He blew on it most deliberately. Nothing like lust for keeping fear at a distance and making time pass.

But nothing would make the time pass.

Hours later cramp woke him with a scream on his mouth. Instantly a hand was thrust beneath his chin, forcing his teeth shut. 'Quiet. Listen,' said several voices. For now at last there was a noise from outside; a tapping from beneath the floor. Oh Zeus, Zeus, make it to be real; don't let it be a dream. There it came again, five taps and then five and then two, just as they had arranged. The darkness around him was full of elbows and knuckles. Everyone seemed to be moving. 'Get back there,' said someone. 'Give us room.' With a great wrenching sound the trap-door came up. A square of lesser darkness – almost, by comparison, of light – appeared at Yellowhead's feet. The joy of mere seeing, of seeing anything at all, and the deep draughts he took of the clean, cold air, put everything else out of his mind for the moment. Someone beside him was paying a rope out through the opening.

'Get on then,' said a voice in his ear.

He tried to, then gave it up. 'I must unstiffen first,' he said.

'Then out of my way,' said the voice. A burly figure thrust itself forward and went hand over hand down the rope and out of sight. Another and another followed. Yellowhead was almost the last.

And so, breathing deep and stretching their limbs, they all stood by the feet of the great wooden horse with the stars above them, and shivered a little in the cold night wind that blew up the narrow streets of Troy.

2

'Steady, men,' said Yellowhead Menelaus. 'Don't go inside yet. Get your breath.' Then in a lower voice, 'Get in the doorway, Eteoneus, and don't let them in. We don't want them to start looting yet.'

It was less than two hours since they had left the horse, and all had gone extremely well. They had had no difficulty in finding the Scaean gate. Once you are inside a city's wall every unarmed enemy is either a guide or a dead man, and most choose to be the first. There was a guard at the gate, of course, but they had disposed of it quickly and, what was best of all, with very little noise. In twenty minutes they had got the gate open and the main army was pouring in. There had been no serious fighting till they reached the citadel. It had been lively enough there for a bit, but Yellowhead and his Spartans had suffered little, because Agamemnon had insisted on leading the van. Yellowhead had thought, all things considered, that this place should have been his own, for the whole war was in a sense his war, even if Agamemnon were the King of Kings and his elder brother. Once they were inside the outer circling wall of the citadel, the main body had set about the inner gate which was very strong, while Yellowhead and his party had been sent round to find a back way in. They had overpowered what defence they found there and now they stopped to pant and mop their faces and clean their swords and spear-blades.

This little porch opened on a stone platform circled by a wall that was only breast-high. Yellowhead leaned his elbow on it and looked down. He could not see the stars now. Troy was burning. The glorious fires, the loud manes and beards of flame and the billows of smoke, blotted out the sky. Beyond the city the whole countryside was lit up with the glare; you could see even the familiar and hated beach itself and the endless line of ships. Thank the gods, they would soon bid goodbye to that!

While they had been fighting he had never given Helen a thought and had been happy; he had felt himself once more a king and a soldier, and every decision he made had proved right. As the sweat dried, though he was thirsty as an oven and had a smarting little gash above his knee, some of the sweetness of victory began to come into his mind. Agamemnon no doubt would be called the City-Sacker. But Yellowhead had a notion that when the story reached the minstrels he himself would be the centre of it. The pith of the song would be how Menelaus, King of Sparta, had won back from the barbarians the most beautiful woman in the world. He did not yet know whether he would take her back to his bed or not, but he would certainly not kill her. Destroy a trophy like that?

A shiver reminded him that the men would be getting cold and that some might be losing their nerve. He thrust through the mass and went up the shallow steps to where Eteoneus was standing. 'I'll come here,' he said. 'You bring up the rear and chivvy them on.' Then he raised his voice. 'Now, friends,' he said, 'we're going in. Keep together and keep your eyes open. There may be mopping up to do. And they're probably holding some passage further in.'

He led them for a few paces under darkness past fat pillars and then out into a small court open to the sky — brilliantly lit at one moment as the flames shot up from some house collapsing in the outer city and then again almost totally dark. It was clearly slaves' quarters. A chained dog, standing on its hind legs, barked at them with passionate hatred from one corner and there were piles of garbage. And then – 'Ah! Would you?' he cried. Armed men were pouring out of a doorway straight ahead. They were princes of the blood by the look of their armour, one of them little more than a child, and they had the look – Yellowhead had seen it before in conquered towns – of men who are fighting to die rather than to kill. They are the most dangerous sort while they last. He lost three men there, but they got all the Trojans. Yellowhead bent down and finished off the boy who was still writhing like a damaged insect. Agamemnon had often told him that this was a waste of time, but he hated to see them wriggle.

The next court was different. There seemed to be much carved work on the walls, the pavement was of blue and white flagstones, and there was a pool in the middle. Female shapes, hard to see accurately in the dancing firelight, scattered away from them to left and right into the shadows, like rats when you come suddenly into a cellar. The old ones wailed in high, senseless voices as they hobbled. The girls screamed. His men were after them; as if terriers had been sent in among the rats. Here and there a scream ended in a titter.

'None of that,' shouted Yellowhead. 'You can have all the women you want tomorrow. Not now.'

A man close beside him had actually dropped his spear to have both hands free for the exploration of a little, dark sixteen-year-old who looked like an Egyptian. His fat lips were feeding on her face. Yellowhead fetched him one across the buttocks with the flat of his sword.

'Let her go, with a curse on you,' he said, 'or I'll cut your throat.'

'Get on. Get on,' shouted Eteoneus from behind. 'Follow the King.'

Through an archway a new and steadier light appeared; lamplight. They came into a roofed place. It was extraordinarily still and they themselves became still as they entered it. The noise of the assault and the battering-ram at the main gate on the other side of the castle seemed to be coming from a great distance. The lamp flames were unshaken. The room was full of a sweet smell, you could smell the costliness of it. The floor was covered with soft stuff, dyed in crimson. There were cushions of silk piled upon couches of ivory; panels of ivory also on the walls and squares of jade brought from the end of the world. The room was of cedar and gilded beams. They were humiliated by the richness. There was nothing like this at Mycenae, let alone at Sparta; hardly perhaps at Cnossus. And each man thought, 'And thus the barbarians have lived these ten years while we sweated and shivered in huts on the beach.'

'It was time it ended,' said Yellowhead to himself. He saw a great vase so perfect in shape that you would think it had grown like a flower, made of some translucent stuff he had never seen before. It stupefied him for a second. Then, in retaliation, he drove at it as hard as he could with the butt-end of his spear and shattered it into a hundred tinkling and shining fragments. His men laughed. They began following his example – breaking, tearing. But it disgusted him when they did it.

'Try what's behind the doors,' he said. There were many doors. From behind some of them they dragged or led the women out; not slaves but kings' wives or daughters. The men attempted no foolery; they knew well enough these were reserved for their betters. And their faces showed ghastly. There was a curtained doorway ahead. He swept the heavy, intricately embroidered, stuff aside and went in. Here was an inner, smaller, more exquisite room.

It was many-sided. Four very slender pillars held up the painted roof and between them hung a lamp that was a marvel of goldsmith's work. Beneath it, seated with her back against one of the pillars, a woman, no longer young, sat with her distaff, spinning; as a great lady might sit in her own house a thousand miles away from the war.

Yellowhead had been in ambushes. He knew what it costs

even a trained man to be still on the brink of deadly danger. He thought, 'That woman must have the blood of gods in her.' He resolved he would ask her where Helen was to be found. He would ask her courteously.

She looked up and stopped her spinning but still she did not move.

'The child,' she said in a low voice. 'Is she still alive? Is she well?' Then, helped by the voice, he recognized her. And with the first second of his recognition all that had made the very shape of his mind for eleven years came tumbling down in irretrievable ruin. Neither that jealousy nor that lust, that rage nor that tenderness, could ever be revived. There was nothing inside him appropriate to what he saw. For a moment there was nothing inside him at all.

For he had never dreamed she would be like this; never dreamed that the flesh would have gathered under her chin, that the face could be so plump and yet so drawn, that there would be grey hair at her temples and wrinkles at the corners of her eyes. Even her height was less than he remembered. The smooth glory of her skin which once made her seem to cast a light from her arms and shoulders was all gone. An ageing woman; a sad, patient, composed woman, asking for her daughter; for their daughter.

The astonishment of it jerked a reply out of him before he well knew what he was doing. 'I've not seen Hermione for ten years,' he said. Then he checked himself. How had she the effrontery to ask like that, just as an honest wife might? It would be monstrous for them to fall into an ordinary husbandly and wifely conversation as if nothing had come between. And yet what had come between was less disabling than what he now encountered.

About that he suffered a deadlock of conflicting emotions. It served her right. Where was her vaunted beauty now? Vengeance? Her mirror punished her worse than he could every day. But there was pity too. The story that she was the daughter of Zeus, the fame that had made her a legend on both sides of the Aegean, all dwindled to this, all destroyed like the vase he had shivered five minutes ago. But there was shame too. He had dreamed of living in stories as the man who won back the most beautiful woman in the world, had he? And what he had won back was this. For this Patroclus and Achilles had died. If he appeared before the army leading this as his prize, as their prize, what could follow but universal curses or universal laughter? Inextinguishable laughter to the world's end. Then it darted into his mind that the Trojans must have known it for years. They too must have roared with laughter every time a Greek fell. Not only the Trojans, the gods too. They had known all along. It had diverted them through him to stir up Agamemnon and through Agamemnon to stir up all Greece, and set two nations by the ears for ten winters, all for a woman whom no one would buy in any market except as a housekeeper or a nurse. The bitter wind of divine derision blew in his face. All for nothing, all a folly and himself the prime fool.

He could hear his own men clattering into the room behind him. Something would have to be decided. Helen did and said nothing. If she had fallen at his feet and begged for forgiveness; if she had risen up and cursed him; if she had stabbed herself . . . But she only waited with her hands (they were knuckley hands now) on her lap. The room was filling with men. It would be terrible if they recognized Helen; perhaps worse if he had to tell them. The oldest of the soldiers was staring at her very hard and looking from her to Yellowhead.

'So!' said the man at last, almost with a chuckle. 'Well, by all the –'

Eteoneus nudged him into silence. 'What do you wish us to do, Menelaus?' he asked, looking at the floor.

'With the prisoners – the other prisoners?' said Yellowhead. 'You must detail a guard and get them all down to camp. The rest at Nestor's place, for the distribution. The Queen – this one – to our own tents.'

'Bound?' said Eteoneus in his ear.

'It's not necessary,' said Yellowhead. It was a loathsome question : either answer was an outrage.

There was no need to lead her. She went with Eteoneus. There was noise and trouble and tears enough about roping up the others and it felt long to Yellowhead before it was over. He kept his eyes off Helen. What should his eyes say to hers? Yet how could they say nothing? He busied himself picking out the men who were to be the prisoners' escort.

At last. The women and, for the moment, the problem were gone.

'Come on, lads,' he said. 'We must be busy again. We must go right through the castle and meet the others. Don't fancy it's all over.'

He longed to be fighting again. He would fight as he'd never fought before. Perhaps he would be killed. Then the army could do what they pleased with her. For that dim and mostly comfortable picture of a future which hovers before most men's eyes had vanished.

3

The first thing Yellowhead knew next morning was the burning of the cut above his knee. Then he stretched and felt the after-battle ache in every muscle; swallowed once or twice and found he was very thirsty; sat up, and found his elbow was bruised. The door of the hut was open and he could tell by the light that it was hours after sunrise. Two thoughts hung in his mind: the war is over – Helen is here. Not much emotion about either.

He got up, grunting a little, rubbed his eyes, and went out into the open. Inland, he saw the smoke hanging in still air above the ruins of Troy, and, lower down, innumerable birds. Everything was shockingly quiet. The army must be sleeping late.

Eteoneus, limping a little and wearing a bandage on his right hand, came towards him.

'Have you any water left?' said Menelaus. 'My throat's as dry as that sand.'

'You'll have to have wine in it, Yellowhead Menelaus. We've wine enough to swim in, but we're nearly out of water.'

Menelaus made a face. 'Make it as weak as you can,' he said.

Eteoneus limped away and returned with the cup. Both went into the King's hut and Eteoneus pulled the door to.

'What did you do that for?' said Yellowhead.

'We have to talk, Menelaus.'

'Talk? I think I'll sleep again.'

'Look,' said Eteoneus, 'here's something you ought to know. When Agathocles brought all our share of the women down last night, he penned the rest of them in the big hut where we've been keeping the horses. He picketed the horses outside – safe enough now. But he put the Queen by herself in the hut beyond this.'

'*Queen,* you call her? How do you know she's going to be a queen much longer? I haven't given any orders. I haven't made up my mind.'

'No, but the men have.'

'What do you mean?'

'That's what they call her. And they call her Daughter of Zeus. And they saluted her hut when they went past it.'

'Well, of all the –'

'Listen, Menelaus. It's no use at all thinking about your anger. You *can't* treat her as anything but your queen. The men won't stand it.'

'But, gates of Hades, I thought the whole army was longing for her blood! After all they've been through because of her.'

'The army in general, yes. But not our Spartans. She's still the Queen to them.'

'That? That faded, fat, old trot? Paris's cast-off whore and the gods know whose besides? Are they mad? What's Helen to them? Has everyone forgotten that it's I who am her husband and her king, and their king too, curse them?'

'If you want me to answer that, I must say something that's not to your liking.'

'Say what you please.'

'You said you were her husband and their king. They'd say you are their king only because you're her husband. You're not of the blood royal of Sparta. You became their king by marrying her. Your kingship hangs on her queenship.'

Yellowhead snatched up an empty scabbard and hit savagely three or four times at a wasp that was hovering above a spilled wine-drop. 'Cursed, cursed creature!' he yelled. 'Can't I kill even you? Perhaps you're sacred too. Perhaps Eteoneus here will cut my throat if I swot you. There! There!'

He did not get the wasp. When he sat down again he was sweating.

'I knew it wouldn't please you,' said Eteoneus, 'but –'

'It was the wasp that put me out of patience,' said Yellowhead. 'Do you think I'm such a fool as not to know how I got my own throne? Do you think *that* galls me? I thought you knew me better. Of course they're right; in law. But no one ever takes notice of these things once a marriage has been made.'

Eteoneus said nothing.

'Do you mean,' said Yellowhead, 'that they've been thinking that way all the time?'

'It never came up before. How should it? But they never forgot about her being the daughter of the highest god.'

'Do you believe it?'

'Till I know what it pleases the gods to have said about it, I'll keep my tongue between my teeth.'

'And then,' said Yellowhead, jabbing once more at the wasp, 'there's this. If she was really the daughter of Zeus she wouldn't be the daughter of Tyndareus. She'd be no nearer the true line than I am.'

'I suppose they'd think Zeus a greater king than either you or Tyndareus.'

'And so would you,' said Yellowhead, grinning.

'Yes,' said Eteoneus. Then, 'I've had to speak out, son of Atreus. It's a question of my own life as well as yours.

If you set our men fighting-mad against you, you know very well I'll be with you back to back, and they won't slit your throat till they've slit mine.'

A loud, rich, happy voice, a voice like an uncle's, was heard singing outside. The door opened. There stood Agamemnon. He was in his best armour, all the bronze newly polished, and the cloak on his shoulders was scarlet, and his beard gleaming with sweet oil. The other two looked like beggars in his presence. Eteoneus rose and bowed to the King of Men. Yellowhead nodded to his brother.

'Well, Yellowhead,' said Agamemnon, 'how are you? Send your squire for some wine.' He strode into the hut and ruffled the curls on his brother's head as if they were a child's. 'What cheer? You don't look like a sacker of cities. Moping? Haven't we won a victory? And got your prize back, eh?' He gave a chuckle that shook the whole of his big chest.

'What are you laughing at?' said Yellowhead.

'Ah, the wine,' said Agamemnon, taking the cup from Eteoneus' hand. He drank at length, put the cup down, sucked his wet moustache, and said, 'No wonder you're glum, brother. I've seen our prize. Took a look into her hut. Gods!' He threw his head back and laughed his fill.

'I don't know that you and I have any need to talk about my wife,' said Yellowhead.

'Indeed we have,' said Agamemnon. 'For the matter of that, it might have been better if we'd talked about her before you married. I might have given you some advice. You don't know how to handle women. When a man does know, there's never any trouble. Look at me now. Ever heard of Clytemnestra giving me any trouble? She knows better.'

'You said we had to talk now, not all those years ago.'

'I'm coming to that. The question is what's to be done about this woman. And, by the way, what do you *want* to do?'

'I haven't made up my mind. I suppose it's my own business.'

'Not entirely. The army has made up its mind, you see.'

'What's it to do with them?'

'Will you never grow up? Haven't they been told all these years that she's the cause of the whole thing – of their friends' deaths and their own wounds and the gods only know what troubles waiting for them when they get home? Didn't we keep on telling them we were fighting to get Helen back? Don't they want to make her pay for it?'

'It would be far truer to say they were fighting for me. Fighting to get me my wife. The gods know that's true. Don't rub that wound. I wouldn't blame the army if they killed me. I didn't want it this way. I'd rather have gone with a handful of my own men and taken my chance. Even when we got here I tried to settle it by a single combat. You know I did. But if it comes to – '

'There, there, there, Yellowhead. Don't start blaming yourself all over again. We've heard it before. And if it's any comfort to you, I see no harm in telling you (now the thing's over) that you weren't quite as important in starting the war as you seem to think. Can't you understand that Troy had to be crushed? We couldn't go on having her sitting at the gate to the Euxine, levying tolls on Greek ships and sinking Greek ships and putting up the price of corn. The war had to come.'

'Do you mean I – and Helen – were just pretexts? If I'd thought – '

'Brother, you make everything so childishly simple. Of course I wanted to avenge your honour, and the honour of Greece. I was bound to by my oaths. And I also knew – all the Greek kings who had any sense knew – that we had to make an end of Troy. But it was a windfall – a gift from the gods – that Paris ran off with your wife at exactly the right moment.'

'Then I'd thank you to have told the army the truth at the very outset.'

'My boy, we told them the part of the truth that they would care about. Avenging a rape and recovering the most beautiful woman in the world – that's the sort of thing the troops can understand and will fight for. What would be the use of talking to them about the corn-trade? You'll never make a general.'

'I'll have some wine too, Eteoneus,' said Yellowhead. He drank it fiercely when it was brought and said nothing.

'And now,' continued Agamemnon, 'now they've got her, they'll want to see her killed. Probably want to cut her throat on Achilles' tomb.'

'Agamemnon,' said Eteoneus, 'I don't know what Menelaus means to do. But the rest of us Spartans will fight if there's any attempt to kill the Queen.'

'And you think I'd sit by and watch?' said Menelaus, looking angrily at him. 'If it comes to fighting, I'll be your leader still.'

'This is very pretty,' said Agamemnon. 'But you are both so hasty. I came, Yellowhead, to tell you that the army will almost certainly demand Helen for the priest's knife. I half expected you'd say "Good riddance" and hand her over. But then I'd have had to tell you something else. When they see her, as she now is, I don't think they'll believe it is Helen at all. That's the real danger. They'll think you have a beautiful Helen – the Helen of their dreams – safely hidden away. There'll be a meeting. And you'll be the man they'll go for.'

'Do they expect a girl to look the same after ten years?' said Yellowhead.

'Well, I was a bit surprised when I saw her myself,' said Agamemnon. 'And I've a notion that you were too.' (He repeated his detestable chuckle.) 'Of course we may pass some other prisoner off as Helen. There are some remarkably pretty girls. Or even if they weren't quite convinced, it might keep them quiet; provided they thought the real Helen was unobtainable. So it all comes to this. If you want you and your Spartans and the woman to be safe, there's only one way. You must all embark quietly tonight and leave me to play my hand alone. I'll do better without you.'

'You'll have done better without me all your life.'

'Not a bit, not a bit. I go home as the Sacker of Troy. Think of Orestes growing up with that to back him! Think of the husbands I'll be able to get for my girls! Poor Clytemnestra will like it too. I shall be a happy man.'

4

I only want justice. And to be let alone. From the very beginning, from the day I married Helen down to this moment, who can say I've done him a wrong? I had a right to marry her. Tyndareus gave her to me. He even asked the girl herself and she made no objection. What fault could she find in me after I was her husband? I never struck her. I never rated her. I very seldom even had one of the housegirls to my bed, and no sensible woman makes a fuss about that. Did I ever take her child from her and sacrifice it to the storm-gods? Yet Agamemnon does that, and has a faithful, obedient wife.

Did I ever work my way into another man's house and steal his woman? Paris does that to me. I try to have my revenge in the right way, single combat before both armies. Then there's some divine interference, a kind of black-out – I don't know what happened to me – and he has escaped. I was winning. He was as good as a dead man if I'd had two minutes more. Why do the gods never interfere on the side of the man who was wronged?

I never fought against gods as Diomede did, or says he did. I never turned against our own side and worked for the defeat of the Greeks, like Achilles. And now he's a god and they make his tomb an altar. I never shirked like Odysseus, I never committed sacrilege like Odysseus. And now he's the real captain of them all – Agamemnon for all his winks and knowingness couldn't rule the army for a day without him – and I'm nothing.

Nothing and nobody. I thought I was the King of Sparta. Apparently I'm the only one who ever thought so. I am simply that woman's head servant. I'm to fight her wars and collect her tribute and do all her work, but she's the Queen. She can turn whore, turn traitress, turn Trojan. That makes no difference. The moment she's in our camp she is Queen just as before. All the archers and horse-boys can tell me to mend my manners and take care I treat her majesty with proper respect. Even Eteoneus – my own sworn brother – taunts me with being no true king. Then next moment he says he'll die with me if the Spartans decide I'd better be murdered. I wonder. Probably he's a traitor too. Perhaps he's this raddled queen's next lover.

Not a king. It's worse than that. I'm not even a free-man. Any hired man, any pedlar, any beggar, would be allowed to teach his own wife a lesson, if she'd been false to him, in the way he thought best. For me it's 'Hands off. She's the Queen, the Daughter of Zeus.'

And then comes Agamemnon sneering – just as he always did ever since we were boys – and making jokes because she's lost her beauty. What right has he to talk to me about her like that? I wonder what his own Clytemnestra looks like now. Ten years, ten years. And they must have had short commons in Troy for some time. Unhealthy too, cooped up inside the walls. Lucky there seems to have been no plague. And who knows how those barbarians treated her once the war began to turn against them? By Hera, I must find out about that. When I can talk to her. Can I talk to her? How would I begin?

Eteoneus worships her, and Agamemnon jeers at her, and the army wants to cut her throat. Whose woman is she? Whose business is she? Everyone's except mine, it seems. I count for nothing. I'm a bit of her property and she's a bit of everyone else's.

I've been a puppet in a war about corn-ships.

I wonder what she's thinking herself. Alone all those

hours in that hut. Wondering and wondering, no doubt. Unless she's giving an audience to Eteoneus.

Shall we get away safely tonight? We've done all we can do by daylight. Nothing to do but wait.

Perhaps it would be best if the army got wind of it and we were all killed, fighting, on the beach. She and Eteoneus would see there's one thing I can still do. I'd kill her before they took her. Punish her and save her with one stroke.

Curse these flies.

5

(Later. Landed in Egypt and entertained by an Egyptian.)

'I'm sorry you've asked for that, Father,' said Menelaus, 'but you said it to spare me. Indeed, indeed, the woman's not worth your having.'

'The cold water a man wants is better than the wine he's no taste for,' said the old man.

'I'd give something better than such cold water. I beseech you to accept this cup. The Trojan king drank from it himself.'

'Will you deny me the woman, Guest?' said the old man, still smiling.

'You must pardon me, Father,' said Menelaus. 'I'd be ashamed – '

'She's the thing I ask for.'

'Curse these barbarians and their ways,' thought Menelaus to himself. 'Is this a courtesy of theirs? Is it the rule always to ask for something of no value?'

'You will not deny me surely?' said his host, still not looking at Helen, but looking sidelong at Menelaus.

'He really wants her,' Menelaus thought. It began to make him angry.

'If you won't give her,' said the Egyptian, a little scornfully, 'perhaps you'll sell?'

Menelaus felt his face reddening. He had found a reason for his anger now : it accordingly grew hotter. The man was insulting him.

'I tell you the woman's not for giving,' he said. 'And a thousand times not for selling.'

The old man showed no anger – could that smooth, brown face ever show it ? – and kept on smiling.

'Ah,' he said at last, drawing it out very long. 'You should have told me. She is perhaps your old nurse or – '

'She's my wife,' Menelaus shouted. The words came out of his mouth, loud, boyish, and ridiculous; he hadn't meant to say them at all. He darted his eyes round the room. If anyone laughed he'd kill them. But all the Egyptian faces were grave, though anyone could see that the minds within them were mocking him. His own men sat with their eyes on the floor. They were ashamed of him.

'Stranger,' said the old man, 'are you sure that woman is your wife ?'

Menelaus glanced sharply towards Helen, half believing for the moment that these foreign wizards might have played some trick. The glance was so quick that it caught hers and for the first time their eyes met. And indeed she was changed. He surprised a look of what seemed to be, of all things, joy. In the name of the House of Hades, why? It passed in an instant; the set desolation returned. But now his host was speaking again.

'I know very well who your wife is, Menelaus, son of Atreus. You married Helen Tyndaris. And that woman is not she.'

'But this is madness,' said Menelaus. 'Do you think I don't know ?'

'That is indeed what I think,' replied the old man, now wholly grave. 'Your wife never went to Troy. The gods have played a trick with you. That woman was in Troy. That woman lay in Paris's bed. Helen was caught away.'

'Who is that, then ?' asked Menelaus.

'Ah, who could answer? It is a thing – it will soon go away – such things sometimes go about the earth for a while. No one knows what they are.'

'You are making fun of me,' said Menelaus. He did not think so; still less did he believe what he was told. He thought he was out of his right mind; drunk perhaps, or else the wine had been drugged.

'It is no wonder if you say that,' replied the host. 'But you will not say it when I have shown you the real Helen.'

Menelaus sat still. He had the sense that some outrage was being done to him. One could not argue with these foreign devils. He had never been clever. If Odysseus had been here he would have known what to say. Meanwhile the musicians resumed their playing. The slaves, cat-footed, were moving about. They were moving the lights all into one place, over on the far side near a doorway, so that the rest of the large hall grew darker and darker and one looked painfully at the glare of the clustered candles. The music went on.

'Daughter of Leda, come forth,' said the old man.

And at once it came. Out of the darkness of the doorway

[The manuscript ends here.]

NOTES TO
AFTER TEN YEARS

I

by Roger Lancelyn Green

This story of Helen and Menelaus after the fall of Troy was started, and the first chapter written in, I think, 1959 – before Lewis's visit to Greece. It began, as Lewis wrote that the Narnian stories began and grew, from 'seeing pictures' in his mind – the picture of Yellowhead *in* the Wooden Horse and the realization of what he and the rest must have experienced during almost twenty-four hours of claustrophobia, discomfort, and danger. I remember him reading to me the first chapter, and the thrill of the growing knowledge of where we were and who Yellowhead was.

But Lewis had not worked out any plot for the rest of the story. We discussed all the legends of Helen and Menelaus that either of us knew – and I was rather 'up' in Trojan matters at the time, as I was writing my own story *The Luck of Troy* which ends where Lewis's begins. I remember pointing out that Menelaus was only king of Sparta on account of his marriage with Helen, who was the heiress of Tyndareus (after the death of Castor and Polydeuces) – a point which Lewis did not know, but seized upon eagerly and used in the next chapters.

He read the rest of the fragment to me in August 1960, after our visit to Greece – and after the death of Joy (his wife). The Egyptian scrap came later still, I think : but after that year Lewis found that he could no longer make up stories – nor go on with this one. It was because of this drying up of the imaginative spring (perhaps the inability to 'see pictures' any longer) that he planned to collaborate with me in a new version of my story *The Wood that Time Forgot* which I had written about 1950 and which Lewis always said was my best – though no publisher would risk it. But this was late 1962 and early 1963 – and nothing came of it.

Naturally it is not possible to be certain what Lewis would have done in *After Ten Years* if he had gone on with it : he did not know himself – and we discussed so many possibilities that I cannot even be certain which he preferred.

The next 'picture' after the scene in the Horse was the idea of what Helen must really have looked like after ten years as a captive in besieged Troy. Of course the classical authors – Quintus Smyrnaeus, Tryphiodorus, Apollodorus, etc. – insist on her divine beauty remaining unimpaired. Some authors say that Menelaus drew his sword to kill her after Troy had fallen, then saw her beauty, and the sword fell from his hand; others say that the soldiers were preparing to stone her – but she let fall her veil, and they dropped the stones and worshipped instead of slaying. Her beauty excused all : 'To Heracles Zeus gave strength, to Helen beauty, which naturally rules over even strength itself,' wrote Isocrates – and as I pointed out to Lewis, Helen returned to Sparta with Menelaus and was not only the beautiful queen who welcomes Telemachus in the *Odyssey*, but was worshipped as a goddess, whose shrine may still be seen at Theraphai near Sparta.

However, the scrap of the story set in Egypt is based on the legend, begun by Stesichorus and developed by Euripedes in his play *Helena*, that Helen never went to Troy at all. On the way, she and Paris stopped in Egypt, and the gods fashioned an imitation Helen, an 'Eidolon', a thing of air, which Paris took to Troy, thinking it was the real Helen. For this phantom the Greeks fought and Troy fell. On his return (and he took nearly as long to get home as Odysseus) Menelaus visited Egypt; and there the Eidolon vanished and he found the true Helen, lovely and unsullied, and took *her* back to Sparta with him. (This legend gave Rider Haggard and Andrew Lang the idea for their romance of Helen in Egypt, *The World's Desire*, though it was set some years after the end of the *Odyssey* – a book which Lewis read and admired, even if he did not value it quite as highly as I do.)

The idea which Lewis was following – or with which he was experimenting – was a 'twist' of the Eidolon legend. 'Out of the darkness of the doorway' came the beautiful Helen whom Menelaus had originally married – Helen so beautiful that she must have been the daughter of Zeus – the dream beauty whose image Menelaus had built up during the ten years of the siege of Troy, and which had been so cruelly shattered when he found Helen in Chapter 2. *But* this was the Eidolon: the story was to turn on the conflict between dream and reality. It was to be a development of the *Mary Rose* theme, again with a twist: Mary Rose comes back after many years in Fairyland, but exactly as on the moment of her disappearance – her husband and parents have thought of her, longed for her, like this – but when she does return, she just doesn't fit.

Menelaus had dreamed of Helen, longed for Helen, built up his image of Helen and worshipped it as a false idol: in Egypt he is offered that idol, the Eidolon. I don't think he was to know which was the true Helen, but of this I am not certain. But I think he was to discover in the end that the middle-aged, faded Helen he had brought from Troy was the real woman, and between them was the real love or its possibility: the Eidolon would have been a *belle dame sans merci* . . .

But I repeat that I do not know – and Lewis did not know – what exactly would have happened if he had gone on with the story.

2

by Alastair Fowler

Lewis spoke more than once about the difficulties he was having with this story. He had a clear idea of the kind of narrative he wanted to write, of the theme, and of the characters; but he was unable to get beyond the first few chapters. As his habit was in such cases, he put the piece aside and went on with something else. From the fragment written, one might expect that the continuation would have been a myth of very general import. For the dark belly of the horse could be taken as a womb, the escape from it as a birth and entry on life. Lewis was well aware of this aspect. But he said that the idea for the book was provoked by Homer's tantalizingly brief account of the relationship between Menelaus and Helen after the return from Troy (*Odyssey*, iv. 1-305). It was, I suppose, a moral as much as a literary idea. Lewis wanted to tell the story of a cuckold in such a way as to bring out the meaningfulness of his life. In the eyes of others Menelaus might seem to have lost almost all that was honourable and heroic; but in his own he had all that mattered : love. Naturally, the treatment of such a theme entailed a narrative standpoint very different from Homer's. And this is already apparent in the present fragment : instead of looking on the horse from without as we do when Demodocus sings (*Odyssey*, viii. 499-520), here we feel something of the difficult life inside.

Books by C. S. Lewis
available in paperback editions
from Harcourt Brace Jovanovich, Publishers

SURPRISED BY JOY
REFLECTIONS ON THE PSALMS
THE WORLD'S LAST NIGHT AND OTHER ESSAYS
THE FOUR LOVES
LETTERS TO MALCOLM: CHIEFLY ON PRAYER
OF OTHER WORLDS
LETTERS OF C. S. LEWIS
THE DARK TOWER AND OTHER STORIES
POEMS
NARRATIVE POEMS
THE BUSINESS OF HEAVEN
ON STORIES: AND OTHER ESSAYS ON LITERATURE
SPIRITS IN BONDAGE
TILL WE HAVE FACES